THE LIMITS
OF VISION

*Other titles by Robert Irwin
published by Overlook*

THE ARABIAN NIGHTMARE

PRAYER-CUSHIONS OF THE FLESH

EXQUISITE CORPSE

NIGHT AND HORSES AND THE DESERT:
An Anthology of Classical Arabic Literature

THE LIMITS OF VISION

Robert Irwin

THE OVERLOOK PRESS
WOODSTOCK & NEW YORK

This paperback edition first published in the United States in 2003 by
The Overlook Press, Peter Mayer Publishers, Inc.
Woodstock & New York

WOODSTOCK:
One Overlook Drive
Woodstock, NY 12498
www.overlookpress.com
[for individual orders, bulk and special sales, contact our Woodstock office]

NEW YORK:
141 Wooster Street
New York, NY 10012

Irwin, Robert.
The limits of vision / Robert Irwin.

Cataloging-in-Publication Data is available from the Library of Congress

Printed in Canada
ISBN 1-58567-460-5
1 3 5 7 9 8 6 4 2

January 10th, 1832. Four days out from Tenerife at 10° 12′ west longitude and 40° north latitude when the temperature was 51.5°, the ship was subjected to a remarkable meteorological phenomenon. During the morning, in the space of some ten minutes, the entire deck of the *Beagle* was deluged with dust and the surface of the sea also, seemingly for a distance of about two hundred yards about our vessel in all directions. Though the dust descended from the sky, the sun was still visible through the pall of dust and, beyond the darkness created by the dust, there were no clouds visible. The descent of the dust was not even and I took pains to observe its passage in its eddies and in the singular patterns it made upon the deck. It is hardly possible to convey the sense of elevated wonder that I experienced as I watched the descent of these particles. However it was rapidly noticed by all that the debris on the deck gave off a sulphurous smell that was anything but heavenly and which added considerably to the distress of those detailed to swab the deck. Indeed until their labours were concluded the whole ship bore a most wretched and unsailorlike aspect and I noticed that the elevation of my spirits gave way to a sense of oppression. The affair was most remarkable and I could not have credited it had I not had ocular demonstration of the same. However I discovered on making enquiry from some of the crew at work on the deck that such visitations are by no means unfamiliar during ocean crossings and the interested reader may find other instances cited in Captain FitzRoy's account of the matter as it was presented to the Admiralty.

The opinion earlier expressed by Chamisso in his *Tagebuch* that such rains of dust may have been collected, conveyed and deposited by whirlwinds should now be discounted for I observed no turbulence in the ship's rigging that could correspond to the proximity of a whirlwind. With the help of Mr (now Captain) Sullivan, I was able to collect a considerable quantity of this dust, weighing a little over four pounds and, when I returned to England some four years later, I was able to have the dust which had been preserved in flasks subjected to analysis under the microscope. The contents of the flasks were shown to be compounded of a considerable variety of materials. Most striking was the presence of a type of fine silicate grit so far thought to be peculiar to the Great Asian Desert of the Gobi. There was also a considerable amount of organic matter such as fragments of the bodies of cockroaches and other insects of the *Blattidae* class as well as cobwebs, fungal spores and even particles of dried blood – whether human or animal it was not possible to determine. By far the largest constituent in these flasks was however common dust such as may be found on the floor of any London household. Captain FitzRoy's suggestion that the dust fall was of volcanic origin, though intelligent, is proved by this analysis to be wide of the mark. The circumstance of common household dust being deposited so far out in the Atlantic is mysterious. Nevertheless it is plainly a manifestation of the material world and partakes of nothing of the supernatural. Here I leave the topic, for we were not subjected to any further manifestations of a similar kind and I was glad to find my interest taking me in other directions.

The Voyage of the 'Beagle', by Charles Darwin (1845)

CHAPTER ONE

I rose and went to the mirror. My name is Marcia. As to what I look like and how old I am, it's all in the mirror. I looked into the mirror and I didn't like what I saw. Flecks of silvery dust and small brown stars doubled the depths of its glass. I scratched tentatively at one of the spots with my nail and the spot disappeared, leaving a thin white plume on the glass like a trail of aircraft vapour. I suppose this was grease from my finger. I dabbed again at the mirror's surface and the ghostly whiteness spread further. I hardly dare to breathe, enthralled by the ectoplasmic stuff that seems to sprout from my medium's fingers. Actually I don't like to breathe on shiny surfaces anyway – it does spoil the shine. I suppose it's the little grits of dust that stick to the condensation.

The horrible messy shapes had spread across most of the surface of the mirror before I could succeed in pulling myself together and could resume scratching, this time strictly with my nail. The glass is so smooth. I really don't know how dust succeeds in clinging to it. It is as if the mirror has a gravitational pull, drawing first the dust, then my face, then the rest of the room into itself. Scratching was no good. I couldn't get rid of all the dust that way. I try my sleeve, but, as I rub and rub, I see that those brown stars are really rust spots, forever unreachable below the surface of the mirror. As to the dust and the grease, well, surgical spirits would really be the thing. I like using surgical spirits. It's not just the smell. I have fancies ...

I fancy that I am in Brazil or Guyana or some place like that.

In Brazil or Guyana or some such place, the simple folk – it is only a few years ago that they toiled in fields made from clearings in the jungle and now they have come to settle in the shanty quarter on the edge of the big town – come to me. They work in hotels, on the railway lines. In the new world they have come to, everything is equally magical – cars, trains, transistors, lights. They treat me as one of them. I live in the shanty town with them, yet it does not occur to them that there may be limits to my healing powers. The white woman's magic is reputed all powerful. Their faces are twisted by a curious mixture of hope and hopelessness. They hope that this evening I will work the miracle cure, but their general situation is hopeless. The magic of the big city is not in general benign. It is the big city they think that has given them that industrial cough, that cancerous lump. I think that they are right. The hut is crowded – the whole family is there, four generations of them. There are many children. The oil lamp that hangs from the low ceiling is rarely still as the heads and shoulders of the men bang against it. The timorous ones gaze at the shadows that are cast by the swinging lamp. They all cover their mouths with their scarves. It is time to begin and reluctantly they shuffle back to give me space to begin my work. I place my hands upon the puckered skin of the patient. I have no instruments and there will be no penetration of the skin by the knife. Instead I begin to call upon the invisible presences, the invisible spirits, the surgical spirits ... Well, I think that using surgical spirits is like that.

By now Philip is really mad with me. There are scarcely breaks in his shouting as it comes staccato up the stairs,

'Marcia, Marcia, Marcia, Marcia! What the hell are you doing? I've got to go now, five minutes ago. Marcia, Marcia ...!'

I look again at the mirror and see epicentres of dust like Magellanic clouds adrift in a void. It would be pleasant, though dangerous, to ... But now the shouting stops and I hear the click of the latch. He is opening the door to go out. I rush downstairs almost tumbling in my haste and cling to him in the open doorway. I do not want him to go and I bury my face on his shoulder, but even as I do so I see that he has his darkest suit on. It must be an important interview. There is quite a bit of dandruff on his shoulder pad. My husband is clad in the night and the stars. Where is the clothes brush? I dare not look for it, for the minute I relinquish my grip he will be gone. Too late anyway. He pulls apart from me.

'I'll be back at six or six thirty at the latest. You could do something to the house. 'Bye now.'

He manages to peck at my face while simultaneously avoiding my clutch and is gone.

Six or six thirty at the latest! That could be seven thirty or even eight. I begin to shake and I sink to sitting on the floor. I look along the hallway. It's all there before me waiting to be done. Though I am afraid, I am still dry-eyed. Indeed the sleepy dust is still in my eyes. The power of my body to generate its own dirt horrifies me. While I sleep, thick brownish grey crystals bubble out in the corners of my eyes.

I wish that I still thought as I thought as a child. That, as I slept, the Sandman tiptoed across the room to my cot, tiptoeing in a curious jack-knifed gait, each pointy knee successively jutting forward, then snapping back. Through closed lids I see that he wears a yellow waistcoat and yellow top hat. He is very thin and a thin smile hovers on his face. I am not old enough to tell whether the smile is benign or mischievous. He dips his long fingers into the glass albarello he carries with him and scatters sleepy dust over my face. It floats on the air and only slowly descends. It will seal my eyes until it is light again ...

I scratch the gunge out of my eyes. Every morning I awake to find waxy dirt in my ears and more earth-like dirt between my toes. At every orifice and crevice of my body I find the dirt congealing. Oh what horror if I should find that it grew from within me!

Now I remember. It is the coffee morning this morning.

CHAPTER TWO

The coffee morning! And if they use the loo upstairs then they may see the unmade bed! They must not see the unmade bed. Be calm. It's hours to go yet. Two hours. I shall make the bed. And try not to think what I shall do after that.

I stand at the end of the bed, patting my cheeks. My skin is still smooth; the sheets before me are wrinkled. I suppose that, as I walk among men and they look at me and see me still pure and youthful (facial exercises and skin-cream actually), as I walk about among them, so pure and youthful, here in the upper part of the house, my secret lies concealed, shut up. It is the bed. It is the ageing monster. Tightly constrained by blankets, it is the bed, hideously creased and riven, that is the passive recipient of my griefs and vices.

It is as if I had spent not one night but eighty years in that bed. I continue patting my cheeks to reassure myself as I look down on it. Most of the ridges run crosswise and I can deduce from this that I spent most of the night pulling myself up on the pillow.

I could be an amnesiac who fears she may have committed a murder the night before. If only she could reconstruct the sequence of events that fateful night, for is that brown mark not a blood stain? If not a blood stain, then what? (By the way, the best thing with blood stains is a soaking and a biological powder. When I scatter flakes of the biological powder on my hand and contemplate their forms, vaguely reminiscent of crystalline snowflakes, I smile for I know that their stillness is deceptive. Locked in these frozen inorganic forms, like so many djinn in so many bottles, millions of living cells are hidden. These flakes pulse with life. I am their mistress, the Snow Queen. The cells wait to be released by the action of water – a single tear might be enough – so that they in turn may release their enzymes. The enzymes descend through the swirling waters to grapple on the strands of fabric with the clotted blood. They crouch over the reddish brown stuff, tearing, chewing, ripping, breaking up the surface of the stain, so that its particles drift towards the surface of the water. I think biological powders are wonderful.)

Still rapt in the sheets, I am also Indian tracker and geologist. I have done nothing about making the bed. Skilled tracker though I am, I can deduce nothing from Philip's side of the bed. The man is an utter enigma, for his side of the bed is quite smooth. Is my husband a man who does not dream? Or does he carefully smooth his half of the bed when he gets up? Every morning when I wake I mean to check but I keep forgetting. It would be strange if he did tidy his half, only his half of the bed. Why should he act like that? As strange as the man with no dreams . . .

Does he fear me? And does he walk like a hunted Indian treading backwards and carefully scuffing out each footprint after he has made it? Yet I am not such a skilled tracker after all, for my eyes travel bewildered over the white wastes. Their Antarctic monotony is broken only by the irregular furrows of the snow dunes and the blood stain, an oasis of dark heat in all this chill. It is windless, and without the wind the formation of these snow dunes is inexplicable. One has the impression that millions of years have gone into their making, but millions of years of what? I do not know. Bemused by these and other mysteries, my eyes travel along the snowy shore, observing the tide-marks and jetsam of the night, but I find no clues that can help to interpret this landscape that lies beneath all reason.

I am sad. It is not only that I am cold and alone, but crumpled linen makes me think of grave cloths. Making the bed makes me think of the laying out of the dead. Let me not think of these last things.

I see it all not successively but simultaneously, so that my broodings on the sheets come together in a composite narrative. The night tide has ebbed from the snowbound desolation. In a house on the edge of the snows someone lies dying. It is the hideous old woman, the wrinkled portrait of evil in the attic. She tosses and writhes in her bloody strait-jacket. For so many years this bed of confinement has been all that she has known; it has been the poor woman's opera. Now it will be her grave. She ceases to struggle. She waits for death and hopes for the Four Last Things. The first spot of blood appears on the sheets.

It is murder. She has been stabbed by the man who does not dream. As she lies there, slowly dying, she struggles to remember how she could so have offended him. She cannot. The man who does not dream meanwhile is making his escape. It is not easy to tread backwards in snow-shoes and he keeps stumbling. In any event he soon realizes that his precautions are useless, for far away, white on a white horizon, he can see his pursuer. I have called her the Queen of the Snows. She is perhaps an avenging spirit in the Eskimo pantheon. Her marvellous hatchet-nosed Indian profile reminds me of a smartly mitred sheet. It is plain that she is a spirit of vengeance, not of compassion, for she has left the victim of the attack to die unattended.

The old woman peers uncomfortably down the length of her strait-jacket. For a long time she sees only pale shades and she is comforted, they seem to beckon her on to a painless oblivion. Then she sees something else. A thin white trickle, very small, scarcely visible, has reached the foot of the bed. These are the enzymes – the snow-ants I call them. Though they have been roused by the smell of blood, they do not hurry, but advance in perfect military discipline. Even so, to the trained observer, the snapping of their mandibles and their saw-toothed claws and the swelling of their poison sacs reveal their eagerness to be at the old woman's fatal wound. The claws of these warrior-ants are truly amazing – out of all proportion to the rest of the body and curving and swelling like pelican beaks. (By the way, to get rid of ants, the best thing is to buy a special powder. The powder is a bit messy, and stamping on them is in a way more effective, but formic acid I have found has a peculiarly nasty smell.)

There is no powder in the attic. The screams of the wrinkled old woman shrill out over the snowy wastes but bring no response. Far away, the crystal-shaped knife of the Queen of the Snows rises and falls over the dreamless man's body. She is hurriedly and clumsily trying to hack out her victim's heart while it is still beating. So the enzymes entered in upon their bloody feast. The ice-woman's knife sparkles in its bloody trajectory. The dreamless man is plunged yet deeper into dreamlessness. The madwoman screams once more. Though I would never call bed-making tedious, still it is something of a chore.

I take a grip and pull the sheets taut. Philip says that I am a bit inclined to let my fancies take a hold of me. It must be true. I do love him when he says things like that. We'll be having the coffee morning in the sitting room. I must get the floor hoovered before they come. I am full of thoughts as I stand back to look at my work. Such as: geologists think that rock folds are important, I suppose, because they are so big and have been there so long. Why shouldn't sheet folds be important because they are small and here only briefly? I should have thought it important to capture the fleeting sheet shapes just because they are so transient. It's all relative, that's what I say (I say it to myself of course; I wouldn't dare say it to anyone else). I mean, to a mite, the creases must appear as enormous mountain ranges, passes and plateaux. The mite lives in the same world as ourselves, yet a different one. It's so difficult for me to say what I mean. I thought I could see some mites on the sheets just now, but they weren't, just white flickers on the edge of vision. My own theory is that the white monotony of the sheets allied to the solitary nature of bed-making tends to produce deceptive visual effects. It is similar to what I have read – I forget where – about members of an Antarctic expedition having all the time the feeling that there was one more member of their party than there actually was.

Actually there are flecks of white on the sheets. I can see them now, but they aren't moving. They must be bits of scurf from the skin. Every flake of scurf will have a tiny army of mites toiling over it – they are that small, but I can't see them. I can only think about them and marvel at their infinite littleness. I marvel at them, but at the same time their silence, their invisibility and their mystery terrify me, but that is by the way. I would never dare mention such thoughts to others. But now, just this morning, for the first time, it occurs to me that others may have similar thoughts and be similarly afraid of speaking. I resolve now to broach the subject at the coffee morning this very day and as I so resolve I am filled with an uneasy fluttering sensation. It would be a fearful thing to talk of. The silence of those tiny mites terrifies me. And I know why. The shapes I have been seeing, the forms that they are taking ...

But no. This business with the sheets, it is only a game I think, something to pass the time while doing something dull. Things are never out of control, though I sometimes play with the idea that they are. Anyway the sheets have all been smoothed out and by now my thoughts have carried me downstairs to the back cupboard and I have the Hoover out. I stand at the end of the hall, one hand on the handle at the top of the casing, the other near the head of the nozzle. I drag it forward like a trainer handling a reluctant mastiff. The hall will have to be hoovered starting from the end nearest the staircase. I press the 'on' switch, revelling as I do so in the power that lies in the touch of a finger. I force the Hoover's head down so that it is made to eat the dirt that lies at my feet. It snuffles and snorts around my ankles. As long as I have the Hoover I know that I have nothing to fear from the dirt. Princess and domesticated monster, we are figures from some mysterious book of emblems. A metal chain connects us. It is not clear to me who is in bondage to whom.

We are halfway along the hall carpet when I realize that, though my dragon still roars and whistles, he is no longer eating the dirt. I kneel to look. The bag is not full. It must be one of the tubes blocked. I dismantle the tubes that lead to the head and poke and blow through them all. It is no use, there is no suction.

Now I begin to shake. My most powerful ally has died on me. (It is true that there is the washing-machine in the bathroom, but though my washing-machine has been useful in the past in detaining, interrogating, even eliminating dirt, I can hardly bring the machine with me as I move from room to room.) I look on the area of the hall carpet that remains to be done. I am still on my knees and on my knees I can feel the draught coming in under the front door. It is perhaps this that accounts for my shaking.

Only a few minutes ago the Hoover was the wise woman's helper. Now, unless I can make it work again, it has joined the enemy, become rubbish. A valued renegade, it will crown one of the rubbish dumps of South London, its hose, curled as a dragon's tail curls, coiled round its heap of untreasure. No Hoover and the coffee morning ladies will be here in less than an hour! Whatever shall I do? At moments like this I wish that someone really helpful would pop in – a sunny smiling neighbour eager for a chat about liquid cleansers while we sip our instant coffee, or a bustling Scottish charlady who is a demon for waxing floors, or an expert from the Institute of Whiteness. I know no such persons. Still I do have other unpredictable visitors. I am sure that my coffee morning 'friends' would be surprised if they met these visitors. Perhaps my visitors may come today and help me with my work ...

CHAPTER THREE

The coffee morning people will come. They must see that not all the carpet has been hoovered. What will they see? Still on my knees, I let my gaze fall from the door to the floor.

Down and down. An old grey carpet, in patches worn down to its foundation of warps and wefts, and beyond the carpet bare boards. I smooth my skirt and bend closer. My face is drawn down to a worn corner of the carpet where only islands of wool remain on a sea of lattice threads. Here there are a hundred islands not of delight but of darkness. Only on some of the islands through the thick wool foliage something glitters and beckons – tiny grits of glass which miraculously survived my last hoovering a fortnight ago, now the glittering fragments have been cast up on the islands. Marooned. Marooned. All is flotsam and jetsam here. I ask myself what it would be like to sail on that darkness and visit those greyly haunted isles.

Others are there before me. Dustballs sail like galleons on the dry sea. From one end of the hall carpet to the other is one hundred and twenty-eight days for an individual dust particle travelling steadily by day and by night. A dustball however can do the journey in less than a week. These apparently unwieldy structures are in fact well designed to catch the draughts that come in under the front door. I marvel at their construction. For instance, the piece of fluff nearest me has a structure based on interlocking helixes. Weaker threads, which coil in looser arabesques, run up and down, linking one curve of the spiral with the next, and serving to trap dust particles and other fragments within the structure.

The strongly coiling helixes are made from human hair – mine and Philip's mostly. The threads without much spring in them seem to come from a dog, though when we last had a dog in the house I really can't remember. Never mind all that now. They are showing me fear in a dustball.

Magnificent though the dustballs are – as complex as a human brain while yet as graceful as a sand-yacht – they are only the crippled and mindless emissaries of their master. Their complex cerebral coils do not allow them to speak. Nevertheless it is plain that they have been sent to summon me. I dare not breathe, watching to see what the dustball's message to me is. Like all others its twisted skeleton is made of human hair and in this case mostly mine. It was a sly joke on the part of the master to send this creature to me – a sly joke or a grim warning.

My hairs cannot be rescued from the thrall of the dustball. They are so fine and the convolutions they have been put through are too intricate. They would snap before I could actually extricate them. The dustball itself teeters for a moment and then succeeds in anchoring itself on the fibres of the carpet. It displays itself to me with all the pride of a herald. Its web gleams and sparkles in the artificial illumination of the hall light. Through the grey fibres of its belly-lining I can just make out an angry core of red fluff, some breadcrumbs, even a couple of pieces of wood. Tendrils of the dustball reach up at me. It means that I am to follow it.

Silently we move off. How can I describe it all? Me with my impoverished vocabulary. For instance only a minute or two ago I described the carpet I kneel on as 'grey'. Now that my eye follows the dustball as it navigates its course between the islands of carpet wool, I see what an inadequate word 'grey' was, for the islands even in this poor light are a riot of greens and ochres and other colours that are unknown to the larger world of nature. Nor is it true that if one lands on one of these islands one will find only grits of glass, for now when I look upon the forests, which like mangrove swamps come down to the edge of sea, those forests which first seemed deserted are in fact aswarm with tiny specks of white dust, thousand upon thousand of them. Sometimes they sit alone; sometimes they come together in shapes vaguely reminiscent of human faces and dance as dust-devils. Further inland in these forests of mystery one sees tendrils of hair raising their necks like dinosaurs. Towering over the rest of the forest they are yet sensitive to the slightest breeze.

And the sea itself! The sea which is not a sea. There are so many sorts of sea down here. Many are like the one we travel on now, fixed and rigid with its waves set in dead matter. But there are other seas which are vast pools of dancing energy. Indeed there are seas within seas, so that within this Sargasso expanse of stagnation there are areas of uncontrollable turbulence. Within the dead sea, other microscopically small seas move, and down here there are philosophies which we know nothing of.

No, I can never describe it all. And in any case I am quite distraught with fear, thinking of my destination. By now the dustball I am following has reached the edge of one of the largest islands. This time the dustball does not so much anchor itself on the coast but wreck itself against it. Marooned, marooned. There are nothing except wrecks that travel in or on this sea.

The dustball can go no further. I am to make my way into the interior alone. I will find other guides shortly. The tresses of the dustball wave as if in farewell – but there are I am sure more complex messages in the pattern of the curving of its tresses, if only I could read that pattern.

Reluctantly I turn to press on through the woollen jungle alone. Rather, my eyes do. It is my eyes, only my eyes, that travel, for my body, my huge and earthy body, lies collapsed on the carpet behind my eyes. I cannot imagine that I shall ever have the power to move my body again, now that the glittering dust is in my eyes. The weirdest thing about my journey now is the silence of the forest. The carpet is alive with activity and its undergrowth rich in smells – old socks and mouse-droppings particularly – but everything in the forest proceeds in perfect silence. Threads are snapping and crumbling into dust, small clouds of bluish gas break free from decomposing fragments of food, mites toil through the pile forest looking for stain pools to browse beside, tiny eggs are being laid and hatched, at every moment more tiny particles of dust descend from the upper air to land in the forest – and all in perfect silence.

Threads from some forgotten fabric loop in vast arches over this part of the forest. Up one of these bridges I can see that a white mite is painfully toiling. It does not know where it is going; its search for decay is random and, since there is no intention behind it, it is perhaps not even a search. My lost eyes follow the mite to the top of the bridge. From here one has a view of some thicker threads lying collapsed below and perhaps what may be a dustball in the earliest stage of its formation. It is a riot of disorder, but a frozen riot, an abandoned dinner-party. It seethes and yet is dead.

At length I perceive another mite at the far end of the bridge of hair. It rears itself up on its stumpy tail. It has been waiting for me. It will be my appointed guide to my meeting in the forest. It stands at the foot of the bridge waving its two blobby white arms. It reminds me of an air traffic controller. And with reason. I am still too high and too distanced from the forest. I must shrink my concerns.

It turns away and I creep behind it. There are more of its friends concealed in the foliage near by. We scurry over the rubble of fibres, paper, earth and cloth. Many of the mites we pass in the forest are actually much smaller than my guide and these little creatures scavenge a living from the leavings of the larger mites.

Here all is in fragments, detached from its origins. And if one comes to one of the roads that run through the forest, one does not follow it, for the roads run nowhere, for these roads have been designed by the principle of evil; that is to say, they have not been designed at all.

At last we come to a clearing in the forest. The floor of this clearing is formed by the thick brown lattice of the carpet's warp and weft. The atmosphere is chill and damp. In the midst of the clearing, I see a huge silvery white coil of wool has succeeded in entwining itself round one of the threads of the lattice. Its serpent sheen is streaked with black, it ripples, and I perceive that it is in some sense or other alive, for its shaking comes from its sporing, and its fibrous stuff spreads all the time a little further around it on the base of the carpet. Closer. Closer and closer. Come yet closer. I see that I have arrived at my destination.

CHAPTER
FOUR
_____

What the Fungus Said
(Doubly misleading perhaps, for it was not the
fungus speaking for itself, but the fungus as
mouthpiece for the Dirt, the Empire of Decay
and Ruin, the Principle of Evil – I didn't know what to call it,
or should it be *them*? Secondly I am not mad. I do not hallu-
cinate. I did not actually hear the fungus speak. Nevertheless
the message of the fungus is as plain to me as if it were actually
speaking.)

ME: Unclean thing! What are you? I conjure you to speak.
THE FUNGUS: For a long time we feared that you would never
descend to join us. Now that you have, you are welcome
and we doubt that you will ever bring yourself to leave us.
ME: Unclean spirit, I call on you again to speak your name.
(*The silkily tressed fungus writhes on its bed of decayed
carpet fibre. It is heavy with spores and reluctant to speak.
Nevertheless at length it speaks.*)
THE FUNGUS: My name is legion.
ME: Hello then, Legion.
THE FUNGUS: Foolish woman! The meaning of 'legion' is that
we are one and yet also many, and therefore it is difficult
for us to speak our true name. But you may call us Master.
At least you will learn to do so.
ME: Ha ha! You'll feel the imprint of my heel upon your back
for this insolence. Ha ha! Why, you are only a little stain of
mildew! My foaming carpet-cleanser will have you out in a
jiffy.
THE FUNGUS: Only a little stain of mildew perhaps, yet a
similar stain on your heart would kill you. In any event,
small white spot though we are, we have been elected to
speak to you on behalf of dust, fermentation, dry rot, iron
mould, the moth, grease, understains, soot, flies, dandruff,
fluff, excrement, bedbugs, mites, rising damp, draught, rust,
stale odours, cockroaches, scorch marks, rattles, creaks,

bangs, cracks, kettle scale, leaks, rips, mice, rats, scratches – in short, the whole *grimoire*. Oh, and as to your much vaunted foaming carpet-cleanser, where do you think that I found the moisture that I need to feed on, if not from your last attempt to clean the carpet with that stuff?

ME: If I were not bored witless, I should not be speaking to you. Nothing can possibly be more trivial than an unhoovered carpet.

THE FUNGUS: You think that because we are small we are trivial? Look around you, please.

(I look and I see the mites reverently making wide circles round the fungus and behind the fungus the iridescent blue of a dead fly's carapace and beyond that the forest set out in clumps of red and green, the tips of its foliage in places discolouring to black and white, and gleaming within the forest brilliantly faceted lumps of grit, and far away on the coastline I can just make out a dustball lurching towards landfall, and beyond that ... beyond that the whispering of the fungus tells me what I cannot see with my own eyes ...)

THE FUNGUS (*continuing*): Where can you go? My empire is tiny but vast. Far beyond your eyeline lies the true horizon which is the skirting board – it is stained, and invisible insects eat out its heart within. Above it your bravely papered walls are mottling. You see, this house is your prison; it will be your tomb.

ME: I can repaper the wall.

THE FUNGUS: You could. You could even repaper the whole house, I suppose, but it is hopeless. All is falling into decay. Even as we talk the dust is falling, the damp is gaining its ascendancy over the fabrics, a thread is giving way and as it gives way the cushion spills out its stuffing which trickles on to the floor and drifts over to join our dark army. Your whole house weeps for you. Trickles of moisture, coal dust, kapok. And even if you could bring yourself to abandon your duties as a housewife and you fled the house, what then? It is worse outside; it is just more grime and dog-shit and torn newspapers. You can walk for the rest of your life without ever coming near to crossing out of the frontiers of the Empire of the Dirt. Go, foolish woman, to the Gobi Desert and see the dust swarms gathered in their armies and cities. Of what avail are you and your (broken) Hoover and your detergents against our master? Go if you must to the deserts of the Gobi and acknowledge the mastery of the Lord of the Dust.

(*Far in the distance a bell rings.*)

ME: I must go. Not to the Gobi, but someone is calling me.

THE FUNGUS: You have our permission to leave. We regret that there are no guides available to show you the way out of the forest. Oh – and don't please think of your departure as an escape. You carry the seeds of your own decay within you. Sooner or later you must come to dust. You will call us Master. In the meantime you may call us Mucor.

ME: I will have you out, Mucor!

I spit on Mucor, so that for a moment my enemy is trapped in my gleaming glob of spittle like a fly in amber. Then I take a hankie from my sleeve and begin to rub furiously. A few spores drift off, but it is useless. The bell rings again. I drop my hankie and my eyes turn to run through the forest, without thinking of which direction they are travelling in.

As the eyes travel they reflect. The forest is thickly populated. What shall explain its wild proliferation of breeds and forms? It was a Victorian anthropologist, I believe, who maintained that 'Dirt is matter out of place.' A thoroughly Victorian and anthropocentric notion, that. Where should dirt be if not on the carpet? Is it not man with his civilizing and cleansing theories the creature who is out of place here? And, to take the argument a little further, is dirt any less dirt when it is in its place in the belly of the Hoover or the dustbin's sack?

No, as far as the carpet is concerned, its *Decay of Species by Means of Natural Failure, or the Elimination of Unfavoured Types in the Race towards Extinction* has yet to be written.

The bell rang again. I cast around seeking to determine from which direction the sound is coming and seeking also to distance myself from the loathsome Mucor – and even in my terror-stricken flight I do not cease to reflect on the scientific problems that the existence of such a jungle will naturally pose to an inquiring mind. For instance one may well conceive that in another and larger world a struggle for survival has imposed a certain discipline of form. Here it is quite otherwise and what the traveller sees is precisely the breakdown of organic forms, all constraint and symmetry being thrown aside. And just as the uniquely twisted skeletal frames of the dust-towers evade conventional scientific terminology, so also human reason is powerless to explain the sequence of events down here. Here everything is totally determined by chance and insignificance, and everything all around lies in a disorder that is repugnant to man. It is for this reason that this jungle has had few explorers. Here nothing is ever repeated; nothing is a consequence of anything. And yet, and yet ... who will not marvel at the antiquity and grandeur of this world for so long veiled from human eyes? I feel a certain unease of the spirit, hard to give name to. It is perhaps because all around me in everything I see things moving towards rest and inertia that I too would like to rest. A great lassitude comes over me. To stay lying on this draughty dirty carpet ... To close my eyes ... To surrender my body to the maggots ...

The bell rings again. It is the third time that the bell has rung. I rise, as from the bottom of some deep black pool. I pull myself up. I stagger half-fainting to the door and pull it open. It is Mrs Yeats.

'Hi! Am I first as usual? You took your time. I haven't come at an awkward moment, have I?'

Stephanie Yeats. She walks straight in, not so much as glancing at the carpet beneath my feet. I stamp about in the hallway and, on the pretext of being shivery, I surreptitiously brush bits of fluff off my jersey. I smile tightly at her. My smile is tight because I remember that I have not cleaned my teeth this morning. Stephanie rattles away, intending I suppose to put me at my ease. Tight-lipped, I rattle back at her lest she suppose that she has caught me at an awkward moment, but at my ankles all this time I hear the whisper of the Fungus. I wonder if Stephanie has the same problems with her carpet as I have with mine?

No, it's plain that Stephanie sees nothing, suspects nothing. She is going on about the cuts in London Transport services. It is as if I were entertaining a deaf and blind person to tea in the middle of a battlefield. But perhaps she does see? Perhaps this is her sang-froid? It's just not the sort of thing one talks about. I don't know.

As I glide away to hang up her coat, she spots the unwashed breakfast things in the kitchen.

'Oh, let me help you with those things before the others come.'

'No!' My 'no' is almost a scream. 'No, it's all right. I actually like doing the washing up. I was saving it to do later.'

Stephanie's eyebrows rise almost imperceptibly. I reach behind me to close the kitchen door, and shepherd her into the sitting room.

Once inside the sitting room Stephanie marches straight across the room. For an instant I play with the notion that she is going to examine the far wall for dust. (It was only yesterday that I noticed that the dust that clings to walls is quite different from the dust that rests on the carpet. The dust that clings to the wall has when one examines it the appearance of a thin vibrant matting. Naturally the coarser heavier bits will drift off to join the rest of the dust on the floor. On the other hand the little specks that are too fine to have been properly attached to the dustballs will float up to find a nesting place on the superficially smooth surface of the wall. On a fine day I have often taken pleasure in observing these transformations taking place in a beam of sunlight.) But no, it is the picture on the wall that Stephanie has gone to look at.

'What a super picture. I'd never really noticed it before.'

The picture is a reproduction of a painting in the Wallace Collection, 'A Woman Peeling Apples' by Pieter de Hooch – a quiet Dutch interior; in the corner of a room the *mevrouw* sits between the sunny window and the glowing fire. There is a basket of apples on her aproned lap and her little girl stands beside her to watch her peel them. The wall is white, the mirror over their heads unblemished, the window has been cleaned and no dust dances in the beams that stream through its closely set panes. There is an open hearth and a fire burning, yet the tiled floor that extends before it is as glossy as a big-budget science-fiction movie. The *mevrouw*, serene in her starched collar and heavy apron, is a vision from the Other World. She hangs over our mantelpiece, my Saviour looking down compassionately upon me.

Stephanie says, 'It's a Vermeer, isn't it?'

'No, it's a De Hooch. You can tell because in Vermeer the tiles of the floor are always at an angle to you, I mean so that they're like lozenges with a pointy bit towards you, whereas in De Hooch the lines of the tiles run away from you like so many railway lines.'

(I've only seen a few Vermeers, but personally I find less to comfort me in his stuff. Things haven't been tidied up properly in his rooms – the table-cloth is usually rumpled and there's a great scatter of things on it, a cup, some letters, some half-eaten fruit and, though the place looks perfectly clean, I always suspect his women of having swept the dust under the carpet.)

'De Hooch! He died mad, didn't he? Gosh! I didn't know that you were into that sort of thing. You should be an art historian. Hey look, you must come with me to the exhibition of feminist art that's opening at the Hayward Gallery this week.'

Mercifully the doorbell now rings again, saving me from having to invent some reason for not going. It is Mary at the door and, before I have finished hanging Mary's coat, Rosemary and Griselda arrive too. I usher Rosemary and Griselda into the sitting room where Mary and Stephanie have already started a wrangle about feminist art. I hurry into the kitchen.

For a few minutes in the kitchen I am on automatic and the robot within me produces the necessary list for the hands to collect – scones, biscuits, small plates, sugar, milk jug, coffee pot. I switch the kettle on and stand contemplating it. It is at this point that I always think, 'A watched pot never boils.' I always think that. It is as automatic as the list of coffee things. It infuriates me.

There are places and activities scattered throughout the house that always provoke in me set and invariable thoughts. Thinking these thoughts humiliates me. I feel that I have been reduced to the level of a dog. Philip was telling me once about some Russian scientist who has proved that dogs always salivate when they hear the sound of a bell. They can't help it. Anyway, as I say, at this point I always think, 'A watched pot never boils.' Not only that but having thought that, I always think, 'I always think that at this point.' It infuriates me. I mean, there must be deep grooves in my head, like when a jelly has set, you can pour a trickle of hot water on its surface and watch the hot water furrow a pathway across the surface of a jelly, and the furrows will remain fixed there even after you have tipped the hot water off.

'At this point I always think that. At this point I always think that.' I suppose that theoretically that sort of thinking could go on for ever. Fortunately somehow I always manage to short-circuit the idiotic internal mumble after only a brief series of repetitions. As now, when I remember my guests. This time I resolve to watch the pot. Perhaps there is some truth in the folk wisdom after all. The point now is that today I am resolved to speak out at my coffee morning. I'm not going to let it drift on without saying what I really think about life and things. On the other hand, though I am nerving myself to this, I am at the same time terrified of what I think I have committed myself to. What will they say? How will they look? Just how awful will the awful silence be?

So I set myself to watch the kettle. My aim is to freeze time. Anything to delay the awful moment. Ah, my Saviour, my frozen icon with peeled apples, let it always be like this, with them in mid-sentence in the sitting room and me here in the kitchen watching a kettle that never boils! For a time, for a long time I think, it seems to me that my wish has been granted and I scarcely dare to breathe. Nothing happens. My face is set in the reflecting gleam of the kettle. Then, like a long exhalation of regret, I hear the faint beginning of the kettle's whistle and its steam dissolves the frozen moment.

I turn to putting honey on buttered scones. I tip the honey-filled spoon and nothing happens. Only awkward seconds later does a thick gob of honey begin to form below the bowl of the spoon and then drop towards the scone. Education has turned me against honey on buttered scones. No one who has read Jean-Paul Sartre's *L'Être et le Néant* could watch me let the honey slowly roll off the spoon without shuddering. If there ever was an immoral household condiment it is honey, sticky, golden, shape-shifting honey. It pretends by turns to be a solid then a liquid! A drop of the stuff falls on my hand. It clings. It wants to be part of me – an extra layer of skin, sticky and viscous. It is soft yet it clings determinedly, so it is like the fungus. If I could, I would breast the world cleanly like a swimmer breaking through water and see the heavens as they really are, but the honey, the fungus, the household dirt, they cover my perceptions like a greasy film. The honey which first, oh so compliantly, filled the spoon, having fallen to the scone spreads over its surface in masochistic self-display. Honey is like a dog who has recognized that he is about to be worsted in a fight and who then turns on to his back to offer his vital organs to the fiercer dog in a ritualized gesture of appeasement. I am filled with revulsion for the cowardly dog who resembles honey and who will live to fight another day. On the other hand, now I come to think of it, I am not sure that I am really any fonder of the fiercer dog, who certainly has no resemblance to honey. Fierce dogs like the one who has just finished contemptuously sniffing the cowardly dog's groin and who seems to be a mongrel with a lot of Alsatian blood in him always make me very nervous. Despondently I return to the business in hand, watching the golden fluid fall and the reflection of my weirdly elongated face trapped in its fall. Then again, I reflect, no one could read Lévi-Strauss's *Le Cru et le Cuit* without identifying honey with menstrual blood and opposing it to tobacco. However the stuff is good enough for a coffee morning and I have in the past noted that smokers do not seem to sense any contradiction between their cigarettes and the scones and honey they are scoffing. By now the two dogs have gone their separate ways and my head is almost on the table, watching the honey spread over the surface of the scones, but I hear sounds behind me. Stephanie and Griselda are in the kitchen. I do not know how long they have been watching me.

'Can we help you carry things through?'

I smile brightly at them. 'Honey on scones for everyone?'

From their gratified expressions I deduce that they have not read Lévi-Strauss's *Le Cru et le Cuit*. We carry through tea things, coffee things, scones and boudoir biscuits. Penny and the rest have been let in while I was in the kitchen. The women in the sitting room form an approximate circle of light, heads bending inwards in innocent communion, faces all smiling, their backs turned to the gathering forces of darkness around them. Flights of conversation pass in all directions like arrows on a muddled battlefield.

'. . . just like a battlefield.'

'. . . so there we were passing this egg-cup round and, as you passed it to the next one, you had to say your name and the name of the person who had just passed it to you. Honestly, I just got the giggles.'

'What lovely scones! They must have taken you ages to make!'

A morning like this is really an occasion for the display of one's housekeeping skills, but one is not supposed to really talk about them. I am supposed to brush the compliment lightly off and move the conversation swiftly on to some new topic – arts, politics, society, whatever. But I do not want to. I want to talk about the passage of time while making scones.

'... a black-belt now, and it's all because she went along thinking that Tae Kwan Do was the Japanese for flower arranging.'

'What you are arguing for is a politics of hysterectomy, isn't it?'

I am unable to speak. My attention is caught by a ball of fluff on Stephanie's skirt and then moves to the folds of the skirt itself. A shallow central valley runs down from the waist to the knees. The gathering of the skirt under her legs creates areas of tension which in turn generate the creases and wrinkles that feed into the central valley, their highlighted ridges and deep shadowed undercuttings simultaneously denying and proclaiming the nature of the fabric.

'I got it at Monsoon.' She laughs nervously. She has seen me staring.

I say nothing. We lack a vocabulary, a notation, for what I am seeing. As it tumbles from the knees the structure of the skirt's folds becomes looser. In loops and whirls and arcs it cascades in glorious complexity. Here is the Great Mystery, for it is as if in the creases of Stephanie's skirt I see the Fingerprint of the Almighty impressed upon her thighs. I find this fingerprint everywhere – the Divine Illiterate, His mark – the mysterious Signature of Things, that leaps from the folds of a rumpled skirt to the grain of an oak tree to the striations of a wind-shaped rock to ash in a deserted fireplace. Now I want to cry out. Ecstasy! Fire! Joy! Look at those creases! Don't move your legs, Steph! Don't speak!

'It was in the sale. Most of the good things were gone, but I got this.'

A brief pause. Is it possible that she in turn is enraptured by the gathered folds of my skirt? But no, it is an essential sign of my grasp on reality that I realize that this is not likely. A thousand dustballs could silently rumble over the carpet towards her ankles and she would not notice them, but they do.

I see them and I understand that she cannot – does not wish to – see them. I am not like Stephanie, but, to use a favourite phrase of hers, I know where she is at. She has shifted her position ever so slightly and with her movement the undulations of her skirt arrange themselves in a new configuration that is random and yet harmonious, and I marvel how the smaller tributary wrinkles conform to the strong pressure of the central cleft between her legs. She is still looking at me very oddly. Not the creases, then. Perhaps she is thinking that I am a lesbian staring at her like this.

'No really, Rosemary, I don't know how you do it. I have enough difficulty writing a letter. Anyway tell us, will it be autobiographical? Eeh hee! You're not going to put us in it, are you?'

'... so he said he was talking about the role of a Christian caring community in South London and I said that I was talking about him coming into my home and behaving like a pantomime cart-horse ...'

'No one's blaming you. Well, it's an accolade, isn't it?'

'I wish I could do something – write a novel, make scones like Marcia's, hang-glide or something.'

Perhaps on the other hand she is a lesbian. It is a funny look she is giving me. Or perhaps, if she is quick as me, she may have deduced from minute indications in my comportment that I have toyed with ideas that she might think me a lesbian and then gone on to consider the alternative possibility ... but no, if she is as deep as all that she will have realized that I do not really think she can be a lesbian, so that this whole unprofitable flight of thought cancels itself out, as if it had never been, but with it the golden moment in the folds of her skirt has been lost.

'... then she came in with him, oh you know, on the lines of would female ordinands be coping people and what would you call them and so on. What about vicarettes, I said ...?'

'... No more than I could count the hairs on his chest, I said, and he had to laugh at that.'

'... You've got to come. Marcia is coming. It's at the Hayward ...'

'... The nature of the guerrilla war in South-east Asia is such that we never really know who the enemy really is and atrocities are bound to be committed by both sides. You can't say that we should judge ...'

'... The point is, where are all the female Rembrandts and Vermeers? The bottom line of all that sort of Dutch painting is men's proprietorial attitude to women. They are possessed, just like the carpets, dogs and fruit-bowls ...'

I take a boudoir biscuit from the plate and I dip it into my coffee and I suck it, eyes closed in concentration. It is a precise psychological experiment which can transport me back to my youth, back to a coffee place opposite the college where I dip a boudoir biscuit into a cup. This movement, this flavour, this texture should be capable of evoking in vivid detail the fall of sunlight over the coffee things all those years ago and the thumb-prints on the copy of a novel that I sat reading as I waited – waiting for Philip to enter the café, waiting for the dreary academic year at college to be over, waiting for the years of preparation to be over when I could assume my chosen role as home-maker and combatant in the struggle against dirt. The smell and texture of the vinyl covering of the table over-heating in the sun ... Two biscuits, two beaded brown surfaces being broken by the dipping biscuits, two Marcias, one looking forward, the other looking back – how should I not be pulled out of the present moment by such an echo of the flavour and sentiment of that exact moment all those years ago? Yet I have to say that nothing of the sort happens for me. Well, I vaguely remember waiting in a café and fretting about Philip and whether I could live only for Philip and become not only a love object for him but also a household object. I can remember that and I suppose the coffee must have been murky brown and the sky must have been blue and so forth, but I have no memory for the precise fall of sunlight through the window across the teacups to illuminate the grubbily thumb-printed novel. What I have is a vague sort of black-and-white memory of something like that made up as much of words as of pictures. I am not transported in a swooning rapture out of time. I am left with my eyes shut in the middle of a coffee morning chewing on a soggy biscuit. The watched kettle of memory has once again failed to boil for me.

'Well, when do you find the time? What is your little secret? Honestly, by the time I have got the kids off to school in the morning ...'

'... not denying that the Open Information Act hasn't made some difference but if you think that now we are going to discover all the secrets about that war you must be very naïve. Too much of it just isn't on paper ...'

My eyes are open now. I am considering my 'friends' around me. What do they look like? To describe them one by one could be tedious. A composite portrait will do. She is English, youngish, middle-class. The eyes are a bit blurred, the hair straggly, no bra or not much of one, sensible shoes, sandals almost. There is a fading bruise on her left cheek which she got from a punch-up with her husband, a skiing fall, from walking into a door, an injection which went wrong, an incident which she is not prepared to talk about. Sit on a park bench and see how long it takes for her to pass by – this woman who is walking away from my coffee morning. My description is a little vague, but no way can you confuse her with Mucor, and that is what matters.

To return to that pale memory of a boudoir biscuit in the café. That was very much a living-room memory. I am a great believer in the orderly storing of memories, to make them easier to retrieve. It is quite a common mnemonic trick. I have a sort of mental image of my house, the House of Memory, and in each room I mentally place certain kinds of thing I want to remember. Generally things are pretty evenly distributed around the house, but as much as one fifth of my store of useful facts is kept in the bathroom. Partly this is because the bathroom is exceptionally well lit and clean, so it is easier to find things in there. Also, it is easier for me to run through all this useful stuff when I am actually in the bathroom, during moments of mental leisure sitting on the loo. Numbers, though, are spaced out evenly around the house. Five is in the kitchen. It is yellow and it hovers in a shimmery sort of way in front of the kitchen window. A green one and a dark blue nine are cramped together in the downstairs lavatory. Two is at the front door, and further along the hallway a black six hangs suspended more or less directly over the spot of fungus on the carpet.

Four and seven are in opposite corners of the living room where I am now silently presiding over a coffee morning. While I am sure we all visualize numbers differently I imagine that there would be a large measure of agreement about keeping four and seven in the living room, for after all they are the numbers of conviviality, aren't they? Perhaps it is this that I should raise now, cutting in on their arguments about the Vietnam War and the display of women in Dutch art. I wish, I really wish, I could pay attention for long enough to what they were saying to be able to participate more fully. Perhaps when they are gone I should get a notebook out and reconstruct from memory as much of their conversation as I can remember. If I made a regular practice of this then perhaps I should be able to set up a file of cards on the sorts of thing that everyone says and from my cards be able to memorize a list of suitable topics to bring into the conversation.

Anyway to go back to the numbers, three and eight are in the dining room across the hallway from the sitting room. I don't know why they are there, unless possibly it is because we keep the TV there as well and Philip and me and the TV makes three, while eight is the maximum number of people we can get round our dining table, but I'm guessing. Tens I keep upstairs in the two bedrooms, the bathroom and on the landing. Hundreds and powers of ten higher are fished out from the jumble in the attic. I see infinity as the cloudy sky rolling over our house. Before I went 'underground' as a housewife, I read mathematics at college (not a very good degree, I am afraid!) but, like many mathematicians who are even better than I am at Boolean algebra and so on, I am not much good at doing quite simple sums of addition and subtraction. So then, when totting up the household accounts, I have found it a help to go up and down the stairs into the various rooms, so as to visualize the figures I am adding up more clearly. It really works! Sometimes though I must admit

I have found myself walking into a room and forgetting what I have come for, an imaginary number or a pair of Philip's socks in the drawer. There are limits to all memory tricks, but still ... I have thought about writing to *Good Housekeeping* about this in the hope of seeing it printed as Tip of the Month.

They are so close in confabulation that their heads almost touch. I stand on the edge tightly smiling (my dirty teeth). The sitting room was done yesterday when I remembered that they were coming. Nevertheless even here, in 'the room for best', the Fungus has its allies. How can they be so oblivious? I am straining to pick up an interchange about men not putting their shoes away, but it is lost. Meanwhile Steph is going on about the feminist exhibition, Griselda and Mary are talking about the new vicar, and the rest are listening to Rosemary being solemn about her bloody novel.

Stuff her novel. Isn't her housework enough for her? It's all so false. In God's name why don't we, why can't we talk about housework? That's all we ever do all day long so it must be important. It is always in our thoughts. We must talk about it, then. I am screwing up my courage to say so. But the truth is that I would rather be anywhere than here and now.

Politics, religion, art, all that high-pitched chatter – they remind me of coolies round a camp-fire, backs to the dark, talking of anything except He whom they fear.

The coolies sit with the soles of their boots showing to the fire. Their eyes are tight slits against the stinging wind. Somewhat shapeless in their fur caps, worn jerkins and wrappings of cloth strips, they are disposed around the fire in a way which reminds me of the tea parties I used to arrange for my dolls when I was a girl. The chief muleteer is holding a stick up in the firelight. The coolie heads come closer together. I cannot see, but I know that on the stick there will be two tiny insects and that the coolies are going to make them fight.

'According to the philosopher Arbus, the Chinese believe that one passes through boredom to fascination.' This is Père Teilhard who has come up behind me while I stood engrossedly contemplating the delight that our workers find in the smallest things.

Père Teilhard is a priest of course. He is also one of the leaders of the expedition and the undisputed authority on the excavation.

'I wish I shared their faith,' I reply. 'How many days have we been here now? And what have we found? And if it's like this now, what will it be like when winter comes ...?' I give an expressive shiver.

'Yes, one always expects a desert to be hot. That is not true of the Gobi, I am afraid.' He speaks softly. 'Yet it must be admitted that even for one like myself who has dedicated his life to work in these unChristian parts, this must be the coldest place in which I have ever had to conduct a dig.'

I look quickly back at him. Does he fear what I fear here at Lop-Nor? The coolies sense it, I know. They have been talking about the earth spirits, how the earth spirits show themselves when disturbed. Faces have been seen in chance arrangements of gravel or carelessly folded linen. The faces can easily be made to disappear with a scuff of the boot. Still they have been seen. And some of the workers have been making surreptitious visits to Dust-Muhammad, the Buryat geomancer who is camped on the other side of the Nor.

The eyes of Teilhard are heavily pouched, the cheeks so cadaverous as to suggest that he has no jaws, and his skin is yellower than any Chinaman's. If I let my eyes drift out of focus, then his face seems to blend in with the sand-laden air around us. Through a freak of turbulence, the air around the camp fire at the head of the crevasse is relatively clear, but everywhere else, all around us, the wind whips up billows of yellow sand and coils of darker subsoil. Even though banks of thick cloud lie between us and the sun, the sky is yellow. A susurrus of grains trickles over our boots. The Bactrians are tethered on the very edge of visibility twenty yards away. Our camels were being loaded with supplies for the geologists' forward camp when this blew up and the chief cameleer (now totally absorbed in urging his insect on) has not troubled to unload them again. The camels strain against their ropes. Some of them, too obstinate to kneel, are lurching dangerously, for their loads which were poorly trussed threaten now to tip them over.

'As to what we have found,' Teilhard continues, 'we have found a great deal. You must admit it. Come to my tent and I will show you what has been turned up today.'

I nod and, throwing up my scarf to cover my mouth and nose, I plod behind him in the yellow storm. The tent is found only by stumbling over its guy ropes. He fumbles at the flaps, then stands aside to let me untie them. We throw ourselves head first into the tent and a great deal of sand follows before the flap can be fastened behind us. For a while there is nothing but darkness and grit. Then the flame of the oil lamp shoots up between the hands of the priest. He forages in his haversack and passes something to me. I take it from him gingerly, expecting it to be one of the day's finds. It is a piece of Sporting and Military Chocolate.

'In France I would never eat chocolate, not even when I was a boy. Every street-corner shop sells the stuff. But here, in the middle of the Gobi, there is something luxurious in the activity – so luxurious, I would almost call it sinful.' Teilhard giggles.

He rummages in his haversack again and hands me something else. I am holding something small but heavy, a shapeless lump – no, not shapeless, for surely nothing is truly shapeless. Soft but heavy. Perhaps its weight comes from the encrustation of dirt? I fetch out my little brush and cloth and begin to work away at cleaning it. This is my skill. That is why I am here. It had not been expected that there would be so much work for me. The expedition was not actually looking for human artefacts. Teilhard's own interest was in scaly lumbering horned beasts who used to lay eggs in sand – whatsitodons or thatsosaurs, some name vaguely reminiscent of a toothpaste ingredient. So the site had been chosen almost at random, a place where the erosive wind had blown away the loess and it would be quicker for us to reach the more ancient strata. Great was our astonishment then when we realized that the trench we had set our coolies to dig was cutting through the midden of an ancient civilization of which even the name was lost. For over a week now we have been digging through or around building rubble, pottery sherds, hearth ash, powder-dry turds. To the eye of the amateur all that we had found was rubbish: to the archaeologist it was gold dust. (I remember Père Teilhard remarking, in a lecture given to the Imperial Academy in Peking, that our view of the ancient preliterate civilizations, not only of Central Asia but also of East Africa, Latin America and elsewhere, had been distorted by the fact that the archaeologist worked largely from the discards and rejects of those civilizations. The museum in Peking was now full of objects which their ancestors thousands of years previously had judged too ugly or too useless to preserve.)

The heavy wind thuds against the tent. The light wavers. I turn the thing round and round in my hands. The priest leans forward anxiously.

'What do you think?'

My reply is slow in coming.

'I don't know. I mean that it's not that I don't know. There is something very powerful in this object ... I sense it. There is an idea in my head but I don't know how to put it into words.' (It is fear as much as anything. It is a little like the fear of ever saying anything truly intimate to casual acquaintances one has invited to one's house.)

Père Teilhard smiles.

'Come, come, Marcia. "Much that is inexpressible would hardly be worth expression, if one could express it." Lichtenberg wrote that. Have you read Lichtenberg? You should, you know.'

'I don't know ... I expect that I'll be clearer about this thing's purpose when I've given it a bit of a rub with my cloth.'

'Perhaps – but I doubt it. You know, I sometimes feel grateful that my vocation has given me insights into our archaeological work that are denied to my lay colleagues. Now is one of those times. Let me tell you, Marcia, something that I worked out for myself when I was a young seminarian. What is a good, or rather goods? (My English is not so good, I think.) I mean those things that we purchase in shops. Why in a Christian society do we call them "goods"? Because these things make us fat, or lazy, or attractive-looking or possessed of status? Surely these are not the properties which make "goods" morally good, are they, Marcia?'

I cannot reply. I am suddenly overwhelmed by the feeling that this is an extraordinarily unlikely catechism to be facing in the middle of the Gobi Desert. And there is something about the object, some half-remembered promise or threat ... *déjà vu* perhaps ...

Teilhard does not notice my distress and continues.

'Ah no, it is because a "good" is something that is good to think with. When we purchase and consume "goods" we internalize them. Goods furnish the building-blocks of our consciousness. Do you understand what I am getting at?

'No? Well, never mind. You will come to it. I have great faith in you, Marcia. Your skills as a housewife have been invaluable to the expedition. Who was it – Emerson perhaps? – who said that genius was an infinite capacity for taking pains? Well, you have that sort of genius.' He sighs. 'You must read Emerson. But what I was leading to now is that this thing there on your palm is not such a commodity. Here is one of the "bads". This is an object which is bad to think with.' The priest looks doubtfully at the lump which is taking on shape in my cleansing hands. 'In truth, I now regret having shown it to you at all. It was foolish of me even to have asked you to come on our expedition. You sense the evil in this thing, do you not?'

I don't know what to say to the priest.

'I ... wouldn't ... I couldn't ever ...' Yes, I am floundering. Perhaps the object in my hands is bad to think with. My thoughts are slow and sticky like jelly in the process of setting, and the boundaries between my words are not as clear as they usually are. And the object is a bit the same. It is not hard. It's a bit pulpy and sticky. It gives way to my inquiring fingers then closes over them, and when I withdraw a finger it feels greasy. It is like being blindfolded and then plunging one's hand into the dustbin in a sort of unlucky dip. Some of the plasticity of a turd, the pulpiness of a large bit of fungus, and yet with some of the sweetly clinging quality of honey mixed with greasy butter. The words in my head are all wriggly but

I know what this thing is and why I am where I am. I have never really forgotten who I face, only I feared to think it in the front of my brain where all is fully lit. All the time we have been sitting in the tent, the knowledge has been resting in a dark untended back room of the brain. Soon it will come lumbering out.

'There is material rubbish and intellectual rubbish. You are holding the former and thinking the latter. *Multo in parvo.*' The priest smiles sallowly, patronizingly. 'Ah, Marcia, I see that you are afraid. It was foolish of me to have persuaded you to come on this expedition – no, selfish rather. You see, we needed you so much. Who but Marcia could have inspired our coolies to cut through so many layers of dirt? Who but Marcia could have kept our trench so tidy? Who but Marcia could have restored our finds to such a shine and made our little patch of wilderness like home? Even so I am sorry, Marcia, for this is no place for a woman.'

I will speak. I will not be silent.

'Father, you did not persuade me to come. I was summoned.'

'Summoned here! How? By whom?'

'I don't know what you call him, Father ... I call him Mucor. He ... it is perhaps the Spirit of Uncleanliness.'

Teilhard crosses himself.

'Merciful heavens, child! And have you seen the Spirit himself?'

'I have and I fear that I shall do so again. It is for this that I was sent. Look here on my hand.'

Bits of grit still cling to the squashy lump which quivers on my palm. Tiny bubbles emerge on its surface and pop. I perceive that Mucor has appeared among these white bubbles. I am dizzy with horror. I can just hear the whisper of Mucor. My swooning vision can hardly hold Teilhard in focus. His pouched and leathery face is merging with the brown wrinkles of the tent's roof. His voice too has become very faint. I can hardly tell one voice from another – and there are other voices ...

'... the source of a very ancient evil, the very well-spring of dirt, the seat of our Prince. It was from here that our Prince conjured up the Black Death and spread it about through the world on the backs of rats and fleas. It was here too that he directed the poisoning of the wells of the nomad herders, thereby transmitting typhoid to the unhygienic kitchens of the West ...'

'Unclean spirit, I adjure you to come out from this woman ...'

'... the numbers of men on earth in each generation increase geometrically, yet the rate of man's increase can never equal the rate of increase of his rubbish. The earth is made of his rubble, the seas are filled with his effluent. Man toils and crawls over his own garbage like an insect ...'

'... Go out from her. Go out, I say!'

'We always fry ours in batter ...'

'... so that walking round the gallery looking at them should be more of a consciousness-raising experience than an aesthetic one ...'

'Marcia, you must go home. I recognize the adversary. This struggle is reserved for the Church, not the housewife ...'

'Our master is outside ... Only let him in and he will bed you in entropy ... Go on, spoil yourself, give yourself a treat, caress yourself ... You deserve it. Relax ... It's time for a break ... Let your hair down and put your feet up ... Comfy? Those are truffles growing under you ... Hard to know where your body ends and the earth you lie in begins. As the body relaxes, it softens, becomes viscous, a bit like cheese fondue really. Delicious, isn't it?'

Though the form of Teilhard is all but dissolved in the murk, yet his insistent whisper breaks through once more.

'Get out, get out, I say! She's ours and I will speak to her ... Marcia, can you hear me? I'm sending you home. Pray for me there, will you? Now listen carefully. Picture a road. Picture a road, woman. Concentrate. Visualize. Don't let yourself go to pieces. That's what Mucor wants. Picture a road. You are walking down that road. On the left-hand side there is a house. Stop and look at that house. It has a minute little garden and a tarmac path going up to the front door. Do you see it, really see it? Good, now. It is your house. Don't let go. Push open the latch of the gate. Only four steps will take you to the door of the house. Take those four steps. The door is green. Its paintwork is blistering. It is unlocked. Push it open and go in. Now you are in the hallway ...'

'Yes.'

Now I can see myself in the hallway, advancing like a sleep-walker. Something white and shimmering on the carpet hisses at my ankles.

'Pay no attention to that. Keep moving, whatever you do. You are in the hallway. Everything about it is sharp and clear. Seven steps will take you to the door of the sitting room. Go into that room ...'

I hesitate, hearing voices through the door, but I go in nevertheless. Only now does the whispering stop. I look back, for I want to argue with the priest. I have not told him what is on my mind.

'I will speak out!' I cry.

'Why, Marcia! Whatever is the matter? You have been in such a brown study! Speak out about what?'

This is Stephanie, who is looking up at me in an amused fashion.

I do not know how I will be able to speak to them politely. Here they sit in my sitting room, exchanging bits of trivia that they have been fed by the newspapers, their husbands or the new vicar, while I am engaged in a struggle against dirt that ranges across all time and space.

Here they sit all cosy with their feet up. Their proper work is quite forgotten and they are grinning and chattering like a gang of Chinese coolies on the skive. The sand is filling the trench that we have dug today and the camels have still not been unloaded. As I watch, the scene around the camp fire is turning ugly. The insects on the stick have stopped fighting and one is mounting the other. The chief cameleer, who has staked much on this combat, whips a knife from out of his jerkin. Pere Teilhard sees me reapproaching and signals me away. Back along the road, the path, the door with blistering green paint.

'Come on, Marcia. What is it? Say it.'

I simulate a vagueness, a bashfulness I do not feel. It all comes out in long jerky breaths:

'No, what I want to say is that here we sit talking about big things that are false to our experience of life – you know, art, religion and so forth, things that really belong to men. Whereas all day, every day, what I am actually doing is folding blankets, washing up and things. I mean the amount of time I actually spend thinking about the role of the woman artist, Steph, is negligible compared to these other things and I'm sure that's true for the rest of us. Even Rosemary's novel takes her less time than the housework.

'Don't all look at me like that. You know perfectly well what I'm getting at. I reckon that I have spent most of my life doing things like watching some gobs of washing-up liquid cut through the grease on a plate and marvelling how that is done and wondering which of the gobs will get to the bottom of the plate first and things like that. So, I just want to say couldn't we please talk about things that we actually know about, like for instance how long it takes a fish-finger to go brown under a grill?'

Silence. The silence lengthens. I look imploringly from face to face. Are they trying to force me to go on and thus fill the silence myself? The silence passes the point up to which one could have pretended not to have noticed anything socially awkward. (Oh, the shame of it!)

At last:

'Well!' Griselda gives a little laugh. 'You could certainly cut the atmosphere with a knife.'

Mary sniffs. 'Excuse me for breathing. Do you want us to go, Marcia? Is this one of your bad days? Is that it?'

'No, of course not.' Actually, no sooner are the words out of my mouth than I realize that that is what I want – for them to go. The force of Darkness is gathering, not just here in my house, but in the houses of all these women, and we sit here sipping coffee and strewing crumbs all over the carpet. It's no use talking to them. They will remain blind to the dangers until Mucor or one of his allies – soot, excrement or grease – actually strikes.

Nevertheless, I reply, 'No, of course not. I just wanted to testify about how I see my life, that's all.'

'My, we are evangelical today!'

Then Steph intervenes with characteristic vigour.

'Oh come on, Marcia! All that daily-beauty-of-domesticity crap is just a role foisted upon us by men.'

'No, Steph. No really. There is something there which they can't see. Actually I wonder if it can really be true that you can't see it either. What do you think about washing up?'

'Whaddya mean, what do I think about washing up? It's boring, messy and it makes my hands come out in rashes.'

Murmurs of agreement all around.

'Oh, can't you see? Can't any of you see? Come on into the kitchen all of you. I'll show you. Follow me.'

And they do follow, coffee cups in hand and whispering amongst themselves.

Now I realize that it is providential that I did not get around to washing the breakfast things earlier. How often previously have I stood here at this sink, doing the washing up and imagining to myself that I was demonstrating my skills here and being admired for them. I have imagined an invisible observer – one who perhaps is initially sceptical of the truths I am trying to teach. And now I have not one invisible observer, but a real circle of baffled housewives. At last it is really happening, my fantasy come true! All it took was courage.

My coffee morning friends stand behind me like the chorus of an ancient tragedy. Red-nailed and raven-locked, the seeress, I look into the waters and prepare to prophesy. The men are away at the wars and a mysterious darkness hangs over our homes.

Streaks of silver run down from the taps. As the hot water begins to come through, tongues of steam lap over the limpid surface. I reach for the power that is mine at the press of a finger. The jet of green spreads through the water in oriental smoke-like curls and then, as I dabble my hands in it, and feel my soul seeping out through my fingers into the water, iridescent bubbles appear seemingly from nowhere, and bubble mounts on bubble. The whole surface of the washing-up bowl is covered with bubbles, all except the patch where I have been dabbling my hands. And when I remove my hands and look down into the bowl, I see this patch as the pupil of an eye looking back at me. The water gurgles, the bubbles wink, and I am filled with joy.

'Would you like me to help with the drying up?'

'No, I just want you to watch.'

The order of things is terribly important. Glasses first, while the washing-up water is still free from grease. I make a couple of glasses thresh in the hot soapy water, rinse them in cold and then dry immediately. It does not do to let glasses drain. They should be brought to a polish immediately. Now I spin round, glasses in hand to show them.

'You see!'

There is complete silence.

Of course I am not really a seeress and I cannot read people's minds. But I do think that one can tell a lot from a person's posture. Stephanie stands erect with her arms folded. She is so erect that she is almost leaning backwards. This means she is above any arguments that I may produce. Her arms are folded against my words. Rosemary sits on one of the work surfaces, her legs wide apart. This posture tells me that she is not at that moment expecting a sexual attack by any male aggressor. (Why it wishes to tell me that I cannot guess.) Griselda on the other hand sits with her legs crossed, showing that, like Stephanie, she is closed to any arguments I may produce – or perhaps I am getting my signs muddled and it is that Rosemary is open to my arguments while Griselda is expecting a male sexual attacker? Only Mary gives me hope. Sitting on the kitchen stool, she is tipped slightly forward and her out-stretched hand covers most of her face. An ambiguous sign. It may be that she fears me and what I am doing, that she is shielding herself against it. On the other hand it may be that what she is trying to cover with that fanning hand comes from within her, for I know and she knows that it is socially taboo to allow excessive emotions, such as awe and reverence, to show publicly. Perhaps in Mary I have found my true disciple.

It could be. There she is, drawn in upon herself, considering
... Washing up is one of love's mysteries. Now she may see
that there is no need to deny one's humanity and become a
robot when one does the washing up, for every action may be
done with loving attention. I am utterly alert to what I am
doing as I plunge the greasy dishes into the almost scalding
water. (The water has to be really hot. I am very tough about
this, like that scene in the film where Lawrence of Arabia
snuffs out matches with his bare fingers.)

Now I spin round to display two plates.

'You see?'

Both dishes shine, but whereas one dish is lustrous from
soap and water, the other is still mottled with the false shine
of grease. I turn swiftly back to the sink to give my audience
time to reflect. Clammy bits of food that have been scraped
from the bottom of the pan flap at my hands under the water,
and the ghostly smell of an old breakfast rises from the sink.
I too am brooding. I need a disciple, for what can I do, a weak
woman and alone, against the power of Mucor? If only I could
make Rosemary understand it too, then she could put me and
Mucor in that novel she is supposed to be writing about
middle-class life-styles and adultery in South London. But then
as I try to imagine myself at my sink in her novel, I realize
how I would feature there.

Marcia's breakdown. Her husband is so often away on business that she is to all intents and purposes living alone, and as
her horizons shrink to the kitchen sink she is going hysterical.
Then, early on in the novel, there is this scene with the ladies'
coffee morning, where Marcia starts raving on about how she
loves washing up and how she wants to tell everyone in the
world about it. Only one person in the group recognizes the
seriousness of Marcia's plight, and that is Rosemary. No, wait
a minute, the names will have been changed. Rosemary is
Rachel, Marcia is Sally, and Philip is Quentin. Later that same
day Rachel/Rosemary rings Sally/Marcia up and invites her to
come round. Sally does and it is the first of many meetings.
With great subtlety Rosemary Crabbe shows how, through the
ministrations and advice of Rachel, Sally the dull little house-

wife is initiated into a way of life that she had not even dreamt of before.

She changes Sally's hair-style, takes her to smart parties and introduces her to Mark. With great subtlety, too, Rosemary Crabbe's first novel shows how the relationship between the two women changes, for as Sally becomes more sophisticated she becomes the dominant one in the pair. Sally begins an affair with Mark, initially with Rachel's blessing. Then, as the affair becomes more serious, Rachel begins to show signs of uneasiness. Mark is a Roman Catholic and tortured with guilt, but what exactly is the source of his guilt? Quentin/Philip sees what is happening, but he is inarticulate and unable to intervene. At a New Year's Eve party in Camberwell, Rachel appears with a young man called Joachim, her brother. That same evening Mark tells Sally that he and Rachel are married but separated, and a little later Sally on her way to the loo stumbles past Rachel and Joachim making love on a sofa. A collage of scenes – wrestling limbs, a picnic laced with barbed dialogue, a fight in a pub, the ride with Quentin in the ambulance after he has taken an overdose of pills, a flashback to the childhood of Rachel and Joachim by the seaside, Sally's flight from Mark and her hopeless attempt to find again the illusory contentment that, she believes, housework and coffee mornings formerly gave her, Rachel's visit to Sally in the mental home and the final Gothic dénouement when Mark takes Rachel and Joachim with him on a visit to his old Oxford college. The men are shown as responding to woman's new liberated role by taking refuge in either impotence or belligerence. Rosemary Crabbe's observation of her characters is deft, and her handling of them compassionate.

I must admit I would like to be in it – for, during the whole long period while I am having an affair with Mark and puzzling over the mystery of Rachel's relationship with Joachim, I don't do any housework, and neither Mark nor Quentin/Philip gets his shirts washed and yet no one seems to notice. That is the new relaxed middle-class life-style for you. But anyway it is all escapism and in real life I shall not leave Philip, and after Rosemary has put me in her novel, she will stop coming to see me because she is embarrassed about it, and Mucor will make her pay for having neglected her housework to write novels. She will pay heavily.

Again I turn. This time both plates are lustrous and, caught in the kitchen's light, their highlights reflect off one another and their mutual reflections seem to me to be a sort of image of infinity and endless mutual devotion.

But now Mary's hand has fallen from her face and I am just in time to detect a hastily disappearing smile. I am furious.

'You are not taking me seriously.'

'Taking what seriously? You are a bloody good washer-up, I'll give you that. Any time you want to come round and do my washing up you are welcome.'

'Oh, that's not the point, Mary. Don't any of you want to communicate? To - to talk about the little things in life, those little things that are so important?'

Their eyes are lowered as if they are looking for little things on the kitchen table. (Well, there are some breadcrumbs there, but I am getting pretty shirty about their unresponsive attitudes.)

Then Stephanie says, 'OK, Marcia. What is it that you want to tell us about them?'

'If you really don't know there's no point in me saying.'

'No, come on, Marcia.'

'We're really interested; I am, anyway.'

A deep breath.

'Oh well, it's things like - like when you go to the lavatory and you've flushed it, have you never tried to race against the noise of the flushing and get out of the bathroom and down the stairs before it has finished, because if you don't the lavatory eats you up in your imagination? Or have you looked at the detergents you are using - how some of them eliminate the dirt, really kill it, while other detergents lift the dirt off from the fabrics, separating but not actually killing the muck? It has quite a psychological effect on me which one I use. It's really interesting. Or how about when you are going to bed and you've switched the standard lamp off in the sitting room and then you are lying in bed and the thought comes to you that you haven't switched that light off and though you know for certain that you have really you have to go down and check because now you have had that thought it must have a purpose, which has to be fulfilled, even if that purpose is making you get out of bed for no reason? Or what about when you are doing the same work, day in day out – washing, cleaning, ironing, shopping and cooking – have you ever thought that every day could really be the same day and it's just that Tuesday gets called Wednesday and then Thursday and so on?'

(A lot of good topics for discussion there, I should have thought. We can get on to Mucor later.)

Complete silence.

I falter, 'Be honest. Haven't you even enjoyed racing drops of water, like these two running down the plate here?'

They stir uneasily like a herd of cattle before a thunderstorm.

Stephanie says, 'You have given me a lot to think about, Marcia. I really must think about it. At our next meeting we must have it all out and discuss it.'

'Yes, this is getting kind of heavy. I think it's time I was going'; and Griselda goes out to look for her coat. The others all troop after her.

'Well, thanks for the coffee and scones, Marcia. I only hope I can produce something half as good when it's my turn.'

'And a very interesting demonstration of how to clean dishes.'

They all nod agreement.

At the door I ask Rosemary, 'Am I going to be in the novel you are writing?'

Rosemary looks embarrassed.

'Writing novels isn't like that. The novelist doesn't put real people in what he or she writes. One takes a gesture from one person, a way of talking from another and the physical features of a couple of other people, say. So it is really a composite character and, of course, there is a lot of the novelist in that character, and then in the course of writing the character develops a personality of its own. So the character is truly fictional and something that is entirely personal to the novelist.'

Liar! I've watched her watching me this morning, mentally noting down my every word and action.

But now they are all gone and I am alone again. Alone, that is, with Mucor.

Well, that's them gone. I am shaking with anger. I go back into the kitchen fuming. The washing up isn't even quite finished yet. One leaves the pans until last and I have real horror to deal with, a saucepan whose bottom is layered by burnt risotto with a covering of last night's cold greasy water. It is very important to give anger its outlet. I know how it can build up. I am going to defuse it in the saucepan. Washing up is a combat situation.

The burnt black stuff at the bottom of the pan, charred stumps, makes me think of a forest in wartime – the Ardennes in 1944 perhaps, and the greasy water lying over it could be dense fog which stops the Allies getting forewarning of the coming German offensive. This scurvy ring higher up the pan could be the level of cloud cover. (It is actually where the rice boiled over – something which should not happen with a risotto.)

Right, I have got this saucepan nicely set up, bending over it like a staff officer in the map room. Let us study this forest. It could be a South-east Asian jungle; then my detergent could be the defoliant the Americans were using. But no, that was an inglorious war and I propose to fight a triumphant campaign. First thoughts were best – it is the Ardennes. The Allies were taken by surprise by the German counter-offensive, as I was when my rice boiled too high and for too long. We now have to re-deploy. The charred rice at the bottom does for the forest – blasted oaks and scorched woody scrub – and also for the German units picking their way through what remains of its cover. Those fragments of rice that have remained white can be seen to be patches of snow turning now to slush in the heavy rains.

There is an odd area in the middle which is a bit greasy, but where the rice has not stuck. That stands for Bastogne. Brigadier McAuliffe is holding out there with the 101st Army Unit. He is saying 'Nuts' to the surrounding burnt risotto. As for me, I am with General Patton's Third Army Corps, hastily moved from the Saar to the relief of Bastogne. Patton is very much a lady's general, I like to think, with his ivory-handled revolvers and his polo ponies, his dash and his swagger – oh yes, and his determination that at all times his men, whether in the Tunisian desert, the dusty Sicilian hills or the Ardennes, should be smartly turned out. Patton had no time for slovens. Not that I knew Patton, of course. He died at the end of the war.

This may all sound silly; I'm sure it does. But I'm a great believer in what some of the magazines I read call 'role models'. They are talking about pop stars and trend-setters in the world of fashion, but I am thinking about the people I read about at school:

– that Spartan boy who kept a fox stuffed up his tunic, and the fox gnawed at the boy's vitals, but the boy never flinched until he died;

– Sir Philip Sidney nobly expiring at Zutphen;

– Captain Oates trudging away from Scott's tent so that his companions' provisions might stretch a few days longer;

– and of course T. E. Lawrence with his matchsticks.

I need to think about people like that to get me through my working day. Their examples act as a pick-me-up when I am feeling low – as now with General Patton for aggression. Shirley Conran hasn't got it: Patton has. And as for treating a pan as a battlefield, isn't that what generals do in real life? According to what I have been told, they sit drunk as stoats in their officers' messes in the evenings moving salt cellars about as if they were tank battalions and tracing rivers on the table by dipping their fingers in the wine. My re-enactment of the Battle of the Bulge is at least getting something useful done.

But enough digressing. I'll get through this faster if I concentrate my forces. Back to the Ardennes. Success = concentration of forces × mobility. I am fully equipped, as one would expect an American army corps to be – nylon brush (my favourite, the motorized section, I think), dish mop, dish cloth, Brillo pad, detergent and tea towel. There is a poised moment when a balance of terror prevails – my terror of getting down to actually doing the pan, balanced against my terror of putting it off and putting it off. At every moment of challenge there is always the possibility that I may walk away from it. But no, a balance of detergence is unreal. The equipment is there to be used.

Get rid of the cold water. The skies are clearing. A tentative scrape with a dry brush. The scouts are being sent out. And now a barrage of hot water, terrorizing and disorientating the enemy, but otherwise inflicting few casualties. When the barrage breaks off, one is amazed by the silence in the woods. No bird sings.

Lost in the forest, my mind begins to wander. What about Patton's ivory-handled revolvers? Ivory goes brown if it is too long in the shadow. His guns will have been all right under the North African sun, but in the Ardennes forest in winter time? I don't like to think of those handles with unsightly brown streaks. It's silly really and it spoils things. I'm not Patton's batman and this sort of thing is wrecking my concentration.

Peering through the water, which is once again greasing over, I imagine the debris of warfare everywhere – abandoned trucks, used cartridge-cases, blanco tins and strands of wire going nowhere. Possibly rubbish tips booby-trapped by the enemy. It seems inconceivable that this place can ever be cleaned up, and the reek of charred corpses is all pervasive. Areas of dirt and cleanliness lie cheek by jowl. The front is fluid, confused. Isolated units of germs stagger about the bottom of the pan. They are the victims of combat fatigue and conflicting rumours. Frantic movement alternates with periods of bored immobility. They cannot believe that Patton could have moved so swiftly. (Patton is, like my Philip, the man of surprises. I never quite manage to get out of Philip what he does in his office all day long. His hours at the office seem to get longer and longer, but every now and again he catches me on the hop by returning home unexpectedly early. This time I must be ready for him, have the house spotless and tidy for my returning warrior. I thought Philip was a man of destiny when I married him. He certainly is a man of mystery.)

Logistics is a matter of attention to detail, making lists and conserving stores. But the preparations and the softening-up operations are over. Now for the attack with all the élan I can give it. The detergent hits the bottom of the pan running. My brush tracks over the same area. Bash! Crump! Thud! Bash! Bash! Bash! Then the storm of steel with the Brillo pad. It is mounted against one of the more weakly defended sectors, forcing the road to Bastogne. And there is fairly concentrated nibbling along a broader front. The germs are rarely seen – only their debris. They are running scared. They are trying to get out of the killing zone, but it is not easy in this waterlogged confusion. Tank tracks churn vainly in muddy lanes. And anyway, which way? The force surrounding Bastogne is itself now beleaguered.

Burnt risotto is easier to deal with than I expected. The germs are operating on extended supply lines and this time Mucor has pushed his *Wehrmacht* a little too far. A final push and the enemy crumbles before the Brillo pad. It is easy to visualize Patton's triumphal cavalcade into the main square of Bastogne. Only mopping-up operations remain. Then I see my face in the bottom of the pan. It is wreathed in a smile of triumph.

That round to me, I think. I am in a thoroughly good humour now and I go out into the hallway to taunt Mucor. Mucor is sullenly silent. Then I catch the smell of stale dish-water on my hands. I should wash them but I haven't had a bath today. I should have a bath.

Slowly, slowly and sinuously, I begin to strip.

CHAPTER SEVEN

Slowly, slowly and sinuously, I begin to strip. As my cast-off garments drop on to the hall carpet, a cloud of dust rises to fondle at my ankles. For a few seconds I pose naked amidst the excitedly flapping tendrils and webs. Then I stride off along the hallway and up the stair. Now there can be no going back, for I did it only to tease and defy Mucor.

Into the bathroom. It's wall-to-wall carpeting in the bathroom. It's one of the great pleasures in my life to wriggle my toes through its thick pile. In a jiffy I have the bath running. Ah now, the water is my friend! We should be allies, for I am, I believe, more than ninety per cent water myself. A nice long soak in the bath and then I must remember to get something out of the freezer for Philip's dinner. (That should not be difficult, for I store my memories of what is in the freezer in the bathroom.) That my body is mostly water, that's scientific. By now I am plunged in water and thought. Yes, that is what I meant to think. That is exactly how I think. I have never got around to telling any of my 'friends' this, but I believe that not only is my body water, but my thoughts and emotions are made of water too. That's how it feels to me. My sympathies just seem to flow out to people and things. On my unimaginative days (fortunately these are very rare) I feel peculiarly dry. At other times however there seems to be an awful lot of water in my head or my heart, and the pressure builds up until it has to discharge – as at the Ardennes. Otherwise I should be springing leaks all over the place. There's no need for me to go on about this, for I can't believe that I'm the only person in the world with plumbing in my brain. I guess that it is the same for all of us; thoughts just swim into our heads, rising up out of depths that we can never fathom. It might even be science. Doesn't psychoanalysis teach us something like that – or have I been misunderstanding what Philip was saying to me again?

Anyway, water in water, I relax in my bath. The bathroom

has recently been repainted green. But on the wall above the bath's taps the rough plaster surface still shows streaks of white. I'm a bit puzzled by this, because I thought that I had been particularly thorough in painting that particular patch; but anyway as I gaze on it, it transforms itself for me into another arctic landscape. The raised bumps of the plaster form cliffs and overhanging crags. Their snow faces fall abruptly to smoother pools of ice below, which have been formed by mysteriously regular streaks of white. Incidentally it's an odd thing, though it does not trouble me, that I see the green as snow, while the white marks are shadows and black ice. I gaze on the tumbling stones and ice and stalagmites. A little to my left I see that there is a cataract; from a rapid of rough stones, shoots of white water fall a prodigious distance to the ice below, and the meeting of the ice and the water produces a froth of steam. Such grandeur on a small scale!

Abruptly I become aware that my bath has become cold. I reach for the hot tap and a renewed stream of consciousness jets down into my bath. The steam clouds cover the arctic landscape, and my eyes unfocus. Since the water at the tap end is getting so hot I draw up my knees. No sooner have I done so than I see that there is space now for a man to join me in my bath. I think it is Leonardo da Vinci. It looks like him anyway – kindly and white bearded with shaggy white eyebrows and a balding head. A bit underfed I think. I reach round him to turn the tap off – I don't know how he can stand it so hot – and then I pass him the soap. He shakes his head. He hasn't got in the bath to wash, but to further the interests of science. On second thoughts he takes the soap from me and watches the soap clouds disperse and dissolve in the water. Then he splashes with his hands to make some ripples and his eyes look intently up at me from under those lovely shaggy eyebrows. What do I make of that?

He wants me particularly to observe the bars of light and shade that the ripples make on the sides of the bath under water. The pattern of the ripples is more accurately registered there. First he makes a pattern – a wave puckered by a central vortex from which a mesh-work of diminishing ripples extends outwards. Then he challenges me to repeat it, that exact pattern, and I find that I cannot. He tries to repeat it and fails also. This is quite exciting, finding myself at the pit-face of scientific research so to speak.

Leonardo believes that there are islands of determinism, of predictability in moving water – call these islands chreods – but they are only islands in its random turbulence. What is this force of randomness that blows through our world, invisible, uncontrolled and leaving only indecipherable patterns to mark its passage? It does not only move through the water. Leonardo points to my thick-pile carpet. There is, perhaps, a faint draught, so that it ripples and billows; and we gaze on it, like two hunters on the edge of a cornfield trying to track the passage of a fleeing animal from the movements of the heads of the corn stalks. We are already breathless from having tracked the creature's passage across the sky, where it left its mark in the shapes of the clouds and the bending of the branches, and down the stream in which the eddies marked its trail. Standing on the edge of the cornfield with Leonardo, I have to take a grip on myself to realize the weirdness of it all. For this is no ordinary hunt, and Force no ordinary animal. He is a spiritual beast and very dangerous. Let me explain. Force is a creature born in the violence of the medieval laboratory. An invisible Frankenstein, Force has been formed by the impact of the animate on the inanimate. The curious thing about him is that the more he is confined and caged the stronger he becomes, until the pent-up strength of Force must inevitably burst from the bars of his cage. So our hunt is curious too, since our purpose is not to catch him, which would only give him more strength, but simply to pursue. This is because the slower Force runs and the more Force senses himself to be corralled in, the stronger he becomes. The faster he goes, the weaker he becomes.

'He will die only in perfect liberty,' says Leonardo sadly. At length we lose the trail. We have lost our quarry and so our hunt is successfully concluded. We must return to the bath, as there will be sweat and ears of corn and burrs to wash off. As I have already noted, Leonardo isn't very bothered about getting clean. However he is as happy as a sandboy at his end of the bath, demonstrating to himself how surface tension creates what is almost a skin on the top of the water. A lovely old man – but quite unaware of the need for bodily hygiene.

Such a handsome old man. Here in the bath I could imagine us making love together with the ripples crashing round us – like in that film *From Here to Eternity*. The roaring waters, our intertwined bodies and the discharge of his desire into me. But then I think isn't that rather dirty, making love in the water one lies in? Like peeing in the sea one is swimming in? This brings me down to reality with a thump (splash?), for I look down and see that the bathwater I am lying in is filthy anyway. I can hardly see my own legs. They look as though they have been pickled in some horrible green fluid. Millions of particles of dirt float like dark stars in the water. It's always the same problem, I find. I clean the house and I get dirty. The bath cleans me and it gets dirty. Then I clean the bath again. Who shall clean the cleanser? And who shall clean the cleanser of the cleanser? It is like using one hand to get sellotape off the other. I could go on for ever about this, but more serious things are afoot. I am for getting out now, but Leonardo restrains me; he wants us to stay in and watch the water going out.

Now we lie squashed together with our heads at the tap end of the bath, but our intimacy is passionless, for all Leonardo's interest is focused on the plughole. First the water swirls in a horizontal plane over the hole. Then a faint declivity appears and this becomes a whirlpool which rapidly extends itself down to the hole. Now Leonardo wants to know why it is that the water is spiralling out. Why does it not simply go straight down the plughole? And why is its spiral anti-clockwise? Impatiently I explain how it is anti-clockwise here and clockwise down in New Zealand. I don't want to stay in the dirty bath a moment longer. However Leonardo shakes his head and twiddles his finger violently round clockwise over the plughole, and now when he removes his finger I see that the spiral has started going round clockwise. This is certainly proving to be a day for surprises!

There is no time for further experiments. The slurping of

the plughole is at its last gasp and sitting back I am uncomfortably aware that my bottom is resting on a residue of bath grit. The last trickle of water runs out under Leonardo's baffled gaze. Leonardo is like me; the most ordinary things are a source of absolute wonder to him. Not taking things for granted, that is the source of his genius and mine. Becoming confidential, Leonardo starts to describe how he finds inspiration for his famous paintings. He likes to look at a wall splashed with stains or made of stones of many colours, and then if he has to invent some new scene, he finds in the stains resemblances to a great number of landscapes adorned with mountains, rivers, rocks, trees, great plains, valleys and hills in various ways. Also battles, and lively postures of strange figures, expressions on faces, costumes and an infinite number of things, which the artist's imagination can reproduce in a more complete form.

By indistinct things, he says, the mind is stimulated to new inventions. He is getting quite worked up about it. I must not take offence, says he, if he now ventures to urge me to stop sometimes and look into the stains of walls, or ashes of a fire, or clouds, or mud, or similar things, for in such things I may find really new ideas. He urges me now to look at the wall behind his head. It is useless for me to protest that I am already very familiar with this practice. He is smiling, but insistent. I must do it now.

I stare then at the wall and as I stare the panic comes upon me, for I am staring at the wall through Leonardo. That smile of his is a crack on the wall (where formerly the arctic landscape had been). Those venerable white hairs are really only streaks of white in the green paint. But the source of my panic is deeper; for, alone now in the bath, as I continue gazing I see that the streaks of white are really colonies of white mildew, and higher up under the window-ledge I see black mildew and finally there in their midst I see Mucor. The silky sheen ripples and it speaks:

MUCOR: Well, here I am again. Your fault; I can't help myself. You got me quite roused out there in the hallway. Go on, put some more water in the bath and I'll come in and join you.

I shake my head in horrified fascination. It is clear that Mucor has his own monstrous version of the *From Here to Eternity* vision. As the surf crashes round us the monster will spore inside me. The exspore of his seed rupturing in my womb, my body will become hostess to his parasitic offspring dividing and multiplying cell into cells and multiplying again and again – until in the end my beautiful white body will look like a mushroom farm.

I scream.

Mucor shakes his fibres at me and continues:

MUCOR: That's what comes of having dirty thoughts.

ME (*shakily*): You can't get it up. You're sexless.

MUCOR (*silkily*): On the contrary, I'm bisexual. Mycology – which is the science of mushrooms – is really a branch of demonology. Every diabolic little mushroom is bisexual, an incubus when he wants to – er – incubate and a succubus when he wants to succubate.

The thought of incubation makes his exospore go rigid with excitement.

ME: You can't get me. You are stuck on the wall.

MUCOR: Perhaps not, but you can come to me. And you will, now or the next time. Your fear of boredom means that you will always be vulnerable to us. You don't fancy me now, but you cannot get away from me. Willy-nilly you will come to know me, and in time the idea of being the bearer of my spores will come to seem quite attractive to you. We'll get you through your understains.

At the word 'understains' I scream again and run still dripping from the bath out on to the landing, down the stairs and into the living room. Ah, my Christ. Where can I turn to for help?

CHAPTER
EIGHT
_____

Dripping and naked, I run into the living room and kneel, gazing up in supplication at the painting that hangs over the mantelpiece. How calm! How cleanly! Like all great art, it is a balm to the soul. My eye is drawn in, in pleasurable contemplation, by the diminishing perspective of black-and-white tiles. I don't know about art critics, but I reckon that most people look at paintings the way I do. I like to imagine myself walking into the picture. It doesn't matter what it is – a painting of an English harvest scene, a feast in a Venetian palace or a mass of pink dots and purple oblongs. I like to imagine myself inside the painting and then, if I like being there, I reckon it is a good painting. It is also nice to imagine how the painting goes on beyond the frame where one can't see. What's more, despite all the stuff that was being talked this morning about 'the formal and ideological bases of feminist art', I reckon all my friends look at paintings the same way too, only they daren't say so. The society I live in is very hypocritical in that way. So many topics are taboo, aren't they? I saw that this morning. One never gets the intimacy from talk that one gets from certain smells. It makes me sick sometimes.

Another thing that is hypocritical is the way my friends go bananas about something in a painting which they wouldn't give a second glance to if it was in real life. I noticed this last night when Philip and I had finished dinner. The dinner things were still on the table – I remember the scooped-out eggshell, almost translucent in the guttering candle-light, and the wax coiling round the base of the candle's stand and the spiral of lemon peel reeling out over the edge of the piled-up dishes and my glass overturned and the lees of its spilt wine mingling with the rose petals from my fading table-piece. I thought it was marvellous. If it had been a painting by Claes van der Heda or Pieter de Hooch we would have been obliged to stand in front of it for at least ten minutes. As it was, Philip just looked irritated that the stuff was still on the table. Dead-eyed. So I just had to clear it away, feeling melancholy for the transience of all things. Why did he marry me? Surely we all see the same world? Why can't we talk about it in the same way? Leonardo was not hypocritical like that.

Not that all this is going on in my head at this moment. Rather, mindful of Mucor at my back, I rush straight into the painting and there I find instant comfort. My God, I could have my dinner off these tiles!

A force stronger than my will draws me to my knees on these gleaming tiles and I run my moist fingers over them, ravished, almost swooning at their tactile values. Amazing! There is not even any dust in the joins between the tiles! This floor must have been gone over with a tooth-comb. (Mind you, if I was going to have my living room painted I'd be jolly sure it was clean too, but still ...) Wonderingly I raise my eyes. The whole room is just so. It gleams and sparkles. No dark shadows anywhere. (If it had been a Leonardo, it would have been full of dark shadows. Shadows fascinate Leonardo. But it is a De Hooch, just the painter to appreciate a nice clean house. Stephanie said something funny about De Hooch this morning. I can't remember what it was now. No matter, it will come back to me.)

What a picture! Once inside, the mind's eye can travel in every direction and have a good look round. The furniture is solid, varnished, dustless – all of it, even down to the fretted cabinet under the table that contains the chamber-pot. The white table-cloth on the table is so dazzling and so sharply creased with starch that it aspires to the condition of cut glass. On it rest not plastic utensils that can be washed by a quick dunk and a rinse, but solid silver and pewter that must be and that have been polished. Just look at the milk churn by the door! It has a handle that shines like gold! Through the open door one can glimpse the garden path running away in diminishing perspective and one knows without having to check that the very bricks of that path have been scrubbed. And the secret of the house – it is from the lips of the child that I learn the secret of the house. The little girl who stands beside The Lady Peeling Apples has been practising her reading, by deciphering the poker-work motto on the fire screen in the corner of the room. The motto from the collected sermons of Pastor Warburg reads, 'God lies in the detail.'

Goodness! And thank goodness that I just had a bath! For it is as if I am in the painting and dripping over this wonderful floor, and the Lady is smiling at me and her eyes following me as I seem to crawl towards her. (I knew that this was a good painting. You can tell when the eyes of the people in the painting follow you.) I am going to tell this Lady everything about myself. It is time to come clean.

And I do. I tell her of my problems with the bed-making and about my archaeological experiences and my conversations with Teilhard and with Leonardo and about the low mentality of the ladies at the coffee morning and how my Hoover has packed up. Nothing is omitted. Above all I tell her of my lonely struggle against Mucor. One may sleep with other people, one may eat with other people, but essentially one does one's housework alone. I am terribly alone.

I am conscious of going on a bit, yet my confession is only a prelude to my inquisition. I want answers from the Lady. Who am I? Why have I been chosen? I am not one of those who go about their work without a second thought, and many questions have come to me as I have stood over the washing-up bowl. In the first place it is extraordinary that I am precisely the housewife that I am. In the second if there are others like me, why do they not reach out and contact me? How is it that I find myself to be the only housewife to whom has been revealed the menace of Mucor and his legions of rubbish? Why have I been chosen?

Lady, you say nothing. Give me answers. Why is it that the world spins around me? That the sun follows me when I walk? That things close to me are large and things distant are small? Why is it that the clouds, the walls, the very grains of dust talk to me and to me alone? There have been poets and painters of vision, but history has not recorded any housewives of vision before my birth. I cannot deny my visions and I sense that I am chosen, yet I feel my visions are a curse that has been laid upon me. Save me from them. At least explain them.

The Brazilian clinic, the washing up, tracing the passage of the invisible beast through the cornfield, one thing after another in my working day and there seems no point to it, just one damn thing after another. And housework is unending. After today's dishes there will be tomorrow's dishes to be washed and dried. Housework is like painting the Forth Bridge. When one has finished it then one knows it is time to start again. But still, when all this is said, I know that what I do has a meaning. Some great mysterious Meaning. What tells me this is something I sense but cannot see. Though it is invisible I know for certain it is there, an invisible audience. As I go about my dusting and sweeping I know that I have an invisible audience. A vast yet unseen audience follows me round the house watching how I do things and it drinks up my thoughts, word by word, image by image. It is for this invisible audience, I think, that I keep this running monologue going on in my head. I have to think loud and clear for them to get it all. I picture this invisible audience as flies upon the wall, thousand upon thousand of them, so closely pressed that some are humped on the backs of others, so many twitching wings and feelers that their presence is almost audible. (Commercially prepared insecticides, by the way, are not much use against the common house-fly, which can rapidly build up an immunity against such products. Personal hygiene and conscientiously performed housework are the best defence against these pests. Flies are extraordinarily filthy in their habits, devouring our food and our excrement quite impartially and paddling their feet in both.) But no, that is all by the way and I mention flies only for comparison, and to make a vivid picture. The truth is that I think of my invisible audience as somewhat closer to human beings than to house-flies.

But why do these invisible creatures watch and listen to me and only to me? Why am I always at the centre of things?

CHAPTER NINE

The whole canvas has been primed; one section of the painting has been executed with such meticulous regard for detail that the pattern of the individual brush-strokes can only be distinguished under a microscope. The general plan of the work, however, is far from clear. Pieter de Hooch is toiling over 'A Woman Peeling Apples'. It is – or rather was – an essay in light; that is, in the controlled modulation of pigment. Light enters from a window high over the woman's left shoulder. Yellow on the glass of the closely leaded casement, it is accurately transcribed by the painter as bluish white where the leaded pattern of light is reflected on the rear wall. The light catches the high domed forehead of the woman, the glittering silver of the sharp knife in her hand, the faint gleam of the golden bowl at her feet. Where the sun catches the highlights of the gilded stucco round the mantelpiece, its super-saturation is expressed in flecks of white pigment. The further from the window the more sombre the colours roused by its fading light, but glowing coals under the bubbling pot provide a secondary source of illumination and spread their gleam over the polished floor tiles. Behind the neatly stacked coals, in the recessed gloom of the fireplace, the existence of a poker is expressed only in silvery threaded streaks.

An exercise in control certainly, in the poised moment. It is late afternoon. Mother and child have the house to themselves for this moment. Soon the men will return, but for this moment the woman is enthroned in control of her environment. In this eerie picture space, this speculative mystery, De Hooch has caught the mystery of housecraft and its transmission from generation to generation. The mother's hand above and the child's below are linked by a shred of refuse; the apple peel falls from the knife into the daughter's eagerly outstretched hand. How many brush-strokes will it take him to create a sliver of apple peel? Each dab of the brush stands for a unit of perception and, prompted perhaps by his work on the apple peel, it seems to De Hooch that he pulls his perceptions out of himself in an endless chain, like a sick man drawing an apparently endless tape-worm out of his mouth.

To have recreated 'A Woman Peeling Apples' as it once was would be a simple exercise in nostalgia. De Hooch is not interested in that. His single-haired brush has already registered the rhizomatic spread of *craquelure* that has afflicted the canvas in its centuries' ageing – and the dust flecks that certainly were not in the original Dutch interior, but which were caught on the canvas when it was photographed. Beyond that, as an additional gloss to the original Delft light of late afternoon, De Hooch's new painting wickedly mimics the bogus shiningness of art in the state of mechanical reproduction. Now he is at work on the mirror over the Woman's head. Half the mirror lies in the direct light of the sun. Hitherto both halves, light and dark, have only reflected bare walls, but presently the grinning painter with his one-haired brush is inserting a tiny, tiny figure in the shadowed half of the mirror, so tiny it is like one of those animalcules he has seen under Cornelis Van Leeuwenhoek's microscope. Indeed De Hooch has to work with a lens to execute the figure. The lens-box duly appears beside the figure and with equally meticulous accuracy the canvas, easel and maul stick. It is a Lilliputian De Hooch that he is painting into the shadows of the mirror.

The next bit is trickier yet. He estimates that the Woman who peels the apples is no larger than his actual hand. She is as seen from a high vantage-point disposed as an irregular solid on the steep perspective of the receding tiles. Now how large should Marcia be? Marcia stands looking at the painting in her living room mid-way between it and its painter. Two Marcias will have to be executed. The first, in the living room, shall be considerably larger than the Woman with her apples. He will catch the colonies of dust that already form on her shoulder-blades and buttocks. (She is of course still naked and slightly wet.) But her face must be seen, and this he will trap in miniature in the mirror. It will be tiny, but still considerably larger than his own.

Marcia is rabbiting on to herself about how what you never

see in these old Dutch paintings is wastepaper baskets or dust-bins and how on earth do they manage? Quite charming, but De Hooch would like a more interesting expression on her face.

He calls out to her, 'Ho, woman! You got dust on your bum!'

That is better. It falls out as he had hoped. She does not turn round. Instead her panicky eyes find him reflected in the mirror. Her hand reaches behind her.

'Oh, you are so dirty!' He roars with laughter. 'Your arse is so dirty!'

Her mouth opens, perhaps to scream.

'No. Do not talk. The woman's talk I do not need when I am at my painting. It is better so. This you I love, I think. I shall have you wet and filthy on my canvas.'

While De Hooch talks, his brush flicks as quickly as his tongue to reproduce the straining of Marcia's tendons as she stands on tiptoe to look at the mirror.

'Dirty, dirty slut! Look there! That good woman has not your modern tricks and devices, but her house is cleaner than yours I think. Look here! I am having to learn new tricks, I, a very old painter. It is a cobweb in the corner of your living room. Never before have I had to paint a cobweb. Look there! You see no cobwebs. Nothing is dirty. The good *mevrouw*, she has rubbed that poker with emery, she has bought Spanish white for the window-panes, the knife is cleaned with Venetian red, she has polished the tiles and she has a pointy stick with which to scrape between the tiles. So it is good. Dutch culture is not germ culture. But you I can hardly see for dirty germs.'

And it is almost true. Tiny translucent creatures, wild yeasts, seem to swim languidly in the film that coats the aged painter's eyes, and smaller spore moulds flicker round the yeasts like erratic tug-boats, and there are still smaller bacteria in that film. De Hooch is, momentarily, a prisoner of his eye for detail. With difficulty he enlarges his vision to encompass Marcia. De Hooch, looking at Marcia, decides to call his painting 'Woman Looking at De Hooch'. Time to get the feel of the woman. Make her flustered; get her moving.

'That cobweb please, I do not like it in my painting. Have you a duster? No need for a chair. I want you to stretch. And there please, crumbs on the floor that your friends have left. Show the dustpan and brush – and your haunches. I want to see those haunches. Now smile at the mirror. No, do not get up. Good so. Now with the duster at the painting. Stretch again. Keep that sulk. I like the sulk. Perfect.'

Marcia's angry body is blushing red all over. De Hooch is now sure that she is a worthwhile subject and continues, 'The worms you despise make a cleaner job of picking a cockroach's corpse than you do of cleaning this room. When your Philip comes home in the evening and finds his living room like this, what does he say! Oh, it is shameful! If you are not here all day to clean, then for what? Pardon me for asking. But your house is not clean and that is not so funny I think. And how long have you to make the whole house clean? From the light in the window it is mid-afternoon. Two hours then maybe. Maybe not so much time. But you must be preening before a great Dutch painter.'

She is almost running now, as she moves around the room, duster and brush in hand. Quite charming. But it is time to catch her in a pose. Have her looking at her master.

'Now stop. Look up at the mirror. Don't try to look back at me. Look at the mirror. Hold that. And what will Philip say when he comes home and finds you like so? No. No talking please. Good girl. Is this how she does her housework, he will be thinking, or has she got some fellow hidden here, some artist type perhaps? Ho ho! What has she been doing all day? It is not cleaning, that is for sure. Wholly not so. Now see how you look. Look into the mirror, and you can see me there too, showing you how you look.'

And De Hooch accompanies these words with curves crudely drawn in the air by his brush and maul stick.

I have looked as he directed and I am doubtful, no longer quite so sure that there is the miniaturized image of an artist in the darkened half of the mirror in the reproduction of 'A Woman Peeling Apples' on my wall. Perhaps there is only a trick of the light. I dab hesitantly at it with my finger and find that there is in fact a bit of gunge adhering to the surface of the glass. Well, it has been a beguiling fantasy while it lasted ... In that it got me through a lot of cleaning in this room. The crumbs from the coffee morning are all gone now, and I should have noticed that half-shred of cobweb before. It takes the eye of an artist to notice such things. De Hooch's voice is stilled. It was never more than noisy thinking, the sort that echoes unbidden in the head when one is very tired. But a touch of nastiness in it that must have come from Mucor. A pity. I was counting on De Hooch to see me through getting the wash done and then giving the kitchen a final tidy before Philip comes home. A failure of the imagination.

As Blake says, 'He who does not imagine in stronger and better lineaments, and in stronger and better light, than his perishing and mortal eye can see, does not imagine at all.'

I say, 'I have had enough of painters for one day.'

'The grubbing Hollanders show only the outer lineaments. That was only Analytics & no true Painting,' Blake replies, and gesturing disparagingly at the bowl and the poker in 'A Woman Peeling Apples', he declaims:

> 'Can Wisdom be put in a silver rod,
> Or Love in a golden bowl?'

'Well, I don't want to be painted in the nude anyway and besides it's getting cold', and I cast around for something to cover my nakedness. His hand on my shoulder stops me.

'No need, Angel, for you are clothed in Light. Besides I shall not paint today. Show me instead, O Angel of the Hearth, a Wonder.'

'Ooh, I know what will interest you. I have been reading about them in Shirley Conran's *Superwoman*.'

I am about to show him some interesting specimens of *Lepisma saccharina* or silver fish. These tiny, brilliantly scaled vermin lurk about under wallpaper, particularly in damp corners. They eat the backing off the wallpaper. Although they are born in damp, when winter comes they look for warmth and move under the wallpaper towards some convenient fire or stove.

But Blake is there before me and recites from his epic poem 'Collembola':

'Lo silver fish
That thread the walls!
Silver fish that eat on paper balls,
Cryptophagic little beasts,
Eating starch, consuming yeast!
Seek out the fire, my little ones,
And find the heat.
For fish to fire must come to fry,
And little fish just burn to die ...'

He breaks off and concludes, 'There is a Wonder indeed.' But darkness passes over his face. 'Angel Marcia, I am come to warn you of your peril. Walk with me thro' to the hallway.'

In the hall Blake has no trouble in finding the mouldy patch on the carpet. This he apostrophizes:

'Mucor, fearsome creature of dust!
Dost think thyself a Thing of Joy?
Shak'st thou thy shaggy spores at us?
Vermin of mould and slime and must!
Vap'rous Horror in the Optic nerve,
Eagerly festering, Satan for to serve.

In a dream when I was sleeping,
I saw a maid with duster in a room.
Maid, I called in tears and weeping,
Or is it Angel? There is your doom.

What is the Hoover but the breath of Man?
And what is mould but death to Kate or Nan?
What is Mould but Death of man?
& what does a Hoover with a broken fan?

'Mucor has been sporting with you,' he continues, 'but when your husband returns, its pipe-play shall cease, yet your body will dance in pain in the wine presses of the mould. Marcia shall be sunken and Mucor risen. Your husband is a man of commonplace reason, and I fear he will think you mad. I hope he will comfort you, yet I prophesy some London hospital's mind-forged manacles and cage. My wild Angel shall be ensnared and when Mucor comes down the ward hissing with delight – '

Mucor, below, hisses with delight. I stamp on him with my heel.

' – you shall be transformed into an Angel of Darkness!'

Now there is a giddy moment when I think Blake is trying to trip me up. It turns out that he wishes to scrutinize the spore-print on my heel. Every fungal spore-print is different. This one is of course household mould. He has got me worried.

'Come off it, William. I'm not mad.'

'You see too much and yet not enough,' he replies gravely. 'Too much for Philip and the doctors, not enough for the Truth. You must see deeper. Your visions should be minutely articulated beyond all that mortal and perishing nature can produce.'

He scrapes something from the wainscoting.

'Look at this atom dancing in my palm.'

I look at the inert speck of dust.

'Can an atom be envious? Are the stars chaste? Are there galaxies that are gluttons? Morality is a matter of scale. Come closer. See smaller. The Gates of Heaven and of Hell open into one chamber. What is dust but atoms? What is a duster but atoms? Dirt and cleanser are one in this Infinite Littleness. The living and the dead are one in this Infinite Littleness. The atoms of the Dead dance as swiftly as the atoms of the Quick and both their dances are holy.'

So then, as I looked on amazed, I saw that the speck was not inert, but it constantly vibrated with the running and the crashing of the electrons and the neutrons, and, seeing that I had seen, the poet recited:

'There is a Grain of Sand in Lambeth that Satan cannot find,
Nor can his Watch Fiends find it; 'tis translucent and has
                                                many Angles,
But he who finds it will find Oothon's palace; for within
Opening into Beulah every angle is a lovely heaven.
But should the Watch Fiends find it, they would call it Sin.

'Mucor's kingdom is not indivisible. So be cheerful, but wary. Is it time for tea?' he breaks off.

'Not yet. Almost an hour to go.'

'Oh. In that case I will be back later. Be Undressed and Ready, My Angel.'

'Goodbye, William!' I cry.

It is always good fun to be with Blake. His visions are quite interesting. But I wish that I understood the half of what he is on about.

CHAPTER
TEN
—————

My coffee morning friends did not even stay long enough for me to get the washing up finished. I am on my way to do it when I notice some grease on the hall wallpaper. The oldest simplest remedies are often the best. I hurry into the kitchen to find some soft white bread and return and set to rubbing at the grease-mark with the bread. Working on a wall, staring close up at it can give a person funny ideas, when they are not concentrated on what they are doing. Young Adolf Hitler was a house-painter. I presume he saw his visions of a Thousand Year Reich in Europe while he toiled over his coats of paint. Since learning about Hitler's early employment, I have worried a bit about the men I let into my house – plumbers, electricians, men to repair the washing-machine, those sort of people. One or two of them have seemed a bit odd to me. No walls to paint: no Hitler. I reckon that walls, drains, biscuit tins, armchairs and pelmets are as much European culture as the grand ideas. The great European novels are inconceivable without ordinary things which we take for granted but which other more primitive parts of the world simply do not have.

I think of the sequel to *The Brothers Karamazov*. Its English title is *The Life of a Great Sinner*. At the end of *The Brothers Karamazov* a jury has found Dmitri Karamazov guilty of the murder of his father, Fyodor Pavlovich. However the reader has been left with the impression that the murder was actually committed by Smerdyakov, son of Fyodor by Stinking Liza. (Smerdyakov was therefore the step-brother of Dmitri, Ivan and Alyosha.) Smerdyakov confessed the crime to Ivan and claims to have done the deed under the intellectual influence of Ivan. Then it seems that Smerdyakov hangs himself.

When *The Life of a Great Sinner* opens we find that fifteen years have passed and the three brothers have taken very different paths. Dmitri had been condemned to twenty years' penal servitude in the mines of Siberia, but, as was planned, his guards were bribed and he and the former prostitute Grushenka succeed in escaping to America. In California, Dmitri finds his fortune as a gold prospector. He and Grushenka become deliriously wealthy.

Grushenka is rather fascinating. I have never knowingly known a prostitute – if you see what I mean – but I gather that it is quite common among suburban housewives. I wonder how one gets started? Maybe one eases into the job by seducing the plumber or the man who has come to look at the washing-machine. I might have asked at the coffee morning. Someone might have known all about it, but it would probably have turned out to be another of those taboo topics . . .

Alyosha has remained true to his decision to leave the monastery and enter the world. To everyone's astonishment, including his own, he marries the young cripple, Lise Khokhlakova. They move away from Skotoprigonyensk and they set up a school for little boys outside St Petersburg. Lise rapidly shows her delight in maltreating and even torturing her charges; in the abasement of his love for her Alyosha is powerless to stop her. However, when the novel opens, Lise has been dead for over a month. (She managed her suicide by throwing a rope over the roof-beam in the schoolroom and, when the noose was secure around her neck, she pushed her wheelchair away from under her. Though her feet still rested on the floor, she spun on the rope, slowly strangling herself. The *dvornik* – that means janitor – finds her in the morning. It seems to be one of the hazards of the job in Russian novels. He has a fit. I mean, really. He has an epileptic fit.)

I must say that I feel a lot of sympathy for Lise Khokhlakova, even though she was a sadist and a child-molester. I sometimes pretend that I am a cripple when I am doing the housework – particularly if there is something to get me going. For instance, if I have got pins and needles in one leg or if I can't see because peeling and cutting an onion have made me cry. Also I sometimes try and do all the washing up one-handed. When I do things like that, the whole house takes on a different shape and things that I had never noticed before become helps or hindrances. Then again I sometimes imagine that the whole house is upside down, and I walk upon the ceiling, and to clean the carpet I stretch on tiptoes and push the hose of the Hoover to its fullest extent, and I have to be careful not to bump into the rigid flex that supports the light bulb. Such things get me out of myself. I gather that the housewives who take up prostitution do it not so much for the pin-money as for the adventure. I identify more with Lise than with Grushenka.

Anyway Lise's suicide. What a terrible thing to have to write about! All very well for a professional novelist like Dostoevsky, but what about Alyosha who has to write round to all his friends and relatives explaining what has happened? One of the people he has to write to is of course brother Ivan, and Ivan has written back from Switzerland telling Alyosha to expect his arrival imminently. Ivan has been touring the spas, scientific institutes and casinos of Europe – the graveyard of culture – and he has had extraordinary meetings with Baron de Rothschild and the French Jesuits.

But, surprise, surprise, it is Dmitri and Grushenka who are first to reach Alyosha and offer him some comfort in his agony of mind. Dmitri has changed his name, grown a beard and masquerades as an American. When Ivan arrives a day later, the three brothers agree that they will go back to their father's house – abandoned but unmolested all these years – and clean the place up. Then they will discuss what must be done in the future. It would be tedious to recall all that happens in the intervening chapters. We now come to the final chapter, called 'Besporyadok', which some translate as 'Chaos' and others as 'Bad Housekeeping'.

Dmitri pushes at the door of their father's house. It is stiff but gives way slowly. Once inside Dmitri kneels and kisses the carpet in the hallway. When he rises from the floor the other brothers notice that his mouth is ringed with dust. The whole house is coated in dust, the dust of Holy Russia. The brothers are resolved that the house shall be set to rights on the morrow, but tonight they are hungry. They have purchased food in Mokroe and, pausing only to give the dusty plates quick wipes with their sleeves, they lay out a feast. During the feast Dmitri gets very drunk and lachrymose. He speaks of Russia's mission to cleanse the world. The Slavs shall sweep over the atheistic West as an apocalyptic cloud of locusts, and the Jews, liberals and Freemasons shall perish in the purging fire of God's furnaces.

Dmitri's extraordinary outburst leads naturally into an argument about who should do the washing up. Alyosha begs to be allowed to do it. 'It shall be the first of my acts of contrition,' he says, but Dmitri and Ivan tell him to sit down. They are determined that Grushenka must do it. Grushenka leans back in her chair.

'I will not. No, never. I want to be so much more than a housewife!' she cries. ' – And so much less. If there were a moujik sitting opposite me, yes, even a moujik far gone with leprosy, I swear to you that I would kneel before that moujik and clean his feet – yes, even with my tongue! But washing plates! No, gentlemen! Washing plates is soul murder. A cleaning woman must be hired. I could be that cleaning woman certainly, but does that make me a dog who cleans the plates for no reward beyond an animal delight in cleaning plates? If you want those dishes done you must pay me.'

Ivan cynically wonders if it might not be more revolting if the moujik had syphilis. Alyosha tries to reason with Grushenka, pointing out that no task is demeaning if it is done in full mindfulness of God.

'My little Alyosha, you have not understood, have you? My point is that washing dishes is not demeaning enough!' Grushenka replies scornfully.

Dmitri has said not a word. Instead he has gone out into the garden and cut himself a branch of birch wood. When he returns he pulls Grushenka to her feet and sets to flogging her. Alyosha tries to interpose himself but is flung brutally aside. Grushenka lies moaning and bleeding on the floor. Ignoring her moans, the brothers settle down to a game of cards. They are all rich – Dmitri from his gold prospecting, Alyosha from his Academy and Ivan from his writings – but they are all agreed that money is so much filth and they gamble madly. Then suddenly they notice that Grushenka has stopped moaning and that she is dead.

Ivan and Alyosha promptly forgive Dmitri and give him the kiss of peace. (They each get a mouthful of carpet dust in exchange.) Then they point out that he must make his escape as soon as possible. They in the meantime will endeavour to erase all traces of the crime and of their meeting – the corpse, the blood stains, the wine spills, the greasy dishes, all shall vanish. Ivan agrees to let Alyosha do the washing up. Dmitri lurches drunkenly out of the door. Ivan is a bit vague about where the broom-cupboard is. Can Alyosha remember? Yes, but first Alyosha must tell him of a vision he had on the night of Lise Khokhlakova's suicide.

That night Alyosha thought that he stood in the Garden of Gethsemane and he stood with two women in front of Jesus. The women have mistaken Jesus for the gardener, since he is coated in earth. They reach out to ask him directions but Jesus gently replies, 'Noli me tangere.' In the horror of his vision Alyosha realizes that Christ in his infinite humility is concerned lest these silly women get the soil of the grave on their fine clean robes. There is a terrible smell in the Garden. Christ points Alyosha to its cause. Everywhere the dead are on the move, some corpses carrying others. The astonished Alyosha sees Smerdyakov carrying the body of Fyodor Karamazov, and the holy monk Zosima carrying the body of Lise. Zosima's body is far gone in corruption and gives off a smell of sulphur – which is the smell of the human soul. Alyosha attempts bravely to assist Zosima with his load, but Zosima offhands him.

'It is because men are mortal and corruptible, that they can have children. If the grain does not die, it cannot bear any harvest. Have you not heard? We are all maggots in the rotting corpse of God the Father. So now, let the dead bury their dead.'

It is only when Alyosha has finished speaking that the two brothers notice that there is indeed a terrible stink in the house. Incredibly Grushenka's body has started to decompose. It is rotting even faster than Zosima's did in the previous novel. It is time to act. They need a sack and some brooms. Ivan and Alyosha rush out into the hallway. The oil lamp swings crazily in their wake. They do not even reach the broom-cupboard, for in the hallway they find Dmitri stretched out dead. They promptly accuse each other of poisoning him. Alyosha thinks Ivan wanted Dmitri's money, and Ivan thinks that Alyosha wanted Grushenka. After furious recriminations they each forgive the other for the crime that they are sure the other has committed. They exchange the kiss of peace, and some residue of carpet grit moves once more along with the saliva.

'Your vision was nothing,' says Ivan laughing nervously. 'I have had many worse. For instance two years ago in Bad Godesburg when I lay in a hotel room sick with a tubercular fever, I found myself gazing at the wallpaper, an endlessly repeating pattern of foliate diamond shapes enclosing flowers in flowerpots – a horrid fancy French or English wallpaper. I found my eyes being pulled this way and that by the silly pattern. The lines flickered like little devils' tails and my right eye wanted to follow them to the right, but my left eye pulled to the left. My head shook with it all. Here was a diamond and there was a diamond and there another! What did it all mean? I ranged this way and that over the wallpaper and in my fever found it to glow and pulse. Then – I do not know how I can explain this to you, Alyosha – I suddenly became aware of something that I am always aware of. No, that's extraordinary! Confound it, you will understand me. There was a whistling sound in my head which I am always aware of without being conscious of it. That is the sort of paradoxical fellow I am!'

Alyosha assures him that he loves him for it.

'No, but let me finish!' cries Ivan. 'Then your love will surely turn to contempt and pity. This whistling was devilish loud and I found that I could hear a pattern to the whistling and that pattern, my dearest brother, was one of flowers in flowerpots enclosed by diamonds. There was nothing in the universe but those infernal flowerpots and diamonds. It all pulsed in my head, the wallpaper and the whistles. The pulses went in and out, each time further in and a little less further out, and I saw that it – that I – pulsed round one small black thing, so small that it could have been a piece of grit, yet so large that I thought that it encompassed the whole universe. With each pulse, against my will, I was being drawn towards that small black thing. It was smaller than me and dirtier than me, but infinite in its dull evil. It promised an eternity of dullness. Surely I am more interesting than all this little dullness, I thought in my fever, but I was certain that it would in fact consume me . . .'

Here Ivan breaks off, for he has noticed at last that he is talking to himself. Alyosha still sits beside him but Alyosha is dead. Looking down the hallway Ivan sees that a trickle of blood has dribbled out of Dmitri's mouth and stained the carpet. In the midst of the bloodstain Ivan notices something small and dark. Perhaps it is the body of a squashed cockroach. It seems to Ivan that there in the body of this crushed insect is the source of all the deaths – Grushenka's, Dmitri's, Alyosha's certainly, but also Fyodor's and Smerdyakov's. It will be the end of Ivan too. Ivan recollects something which Alyosha has told him of the teachings of Father Zosima:

'God has planted seeds from other worlds in our world and everything that could grow in it does grow in it – but those things are alive only through the sustenance afforded by the seeds from those other mysterious worlds.'

Looking down on the carpet, it seems to Ivan that he does indeed gaze down on one of those mysterious worlds. It is ruled by its own laws and they are laws which shall forever be hidden from common humanity. His heart beating wildly, Ivan looks down on this carpet like God contemplating His Creation. He does not like it. It is filthy and bloodstained. 'What is Hell?' he muses. 'It is, I now maintain, God's suffering at being unable to love His own Creation.' Detachedly he observes that even within the entrails of the long-dead cockroach there is a tiny growth of mould. Crazily he addresses this mould:

'And who are you?'

The reply comes back from the floor:

'Mucor Karamazov, the fifth and most sinful of the sons of Fyodor Pavlovich Karamazov.' Then, even as Ivan tumbles towards it, it adds as an afterthought, 'Down with the Karamazovs!'

I must say I rather agree with Mucor. When I was a student I read these cockamamie Russian novels, like lots of my friends, and I spent weeks at a stretch under their influence wondering why I shouldn't commit suicide. (I only wish that I had the time now – to think of committing suicide, or for that matter to read a long Russian novel.) What I enjoy reading these days, when I have the time, are those books which tell you how to be a wonderful housewife. I do think that my friends have a rather narrow idea of what literature is; novels, plays, poetry, anything apart from that is not literature. Not of course that I think all the manuals on how to run a home are great literature, but some are definitely underrated.

I think that I know the list of simple do's and dont's given at the beginning of M. Baxter's *Adventures in Housekeeping* by heart. Here they are, as well as I can remember them:

1. Enjoy your work; the work is easier to do if you enjoy it. If you do not find that you are enjoying cleaning your house ask yourself if you are doing the right job.

2. Organize your day. It is a good idea to draw up a plan and tick things off when you have done them. Better yet make a chart with all the hours of the day squared off. Then fill in the squares as the tasks allotted to each hour are done. Gaily coloured crayons can be used.

3. Try to do most of the housework in the morning when you are at your best. That way you can have some of the rest of the day to yourself.

4. Always wear rubber gloves.

5. Avoid wasteful motion. Genius economizes and finds new uses for old material.

6. Make sure the equipment you buy is suitable for the use for which it is intended.

7. There are various kinds of dirt. How you get rid of it will depend on the kind of dirt it is.

8. If you have a problem regarding the cleaning of your house,

whether in regard to the dirt or in regard to the equipment needed to remove it, go to a reputable dealer or qualified authority. He will be only too pleased to help.

9. Be safety-conscious. Do you have exposed wiring, dangerous medicines or loose carpet-fittings in your house? The old, the young and the drunk are all at risk from these things. Keep them out of your house.

10. Be economical. In cases where a cheaper cleanser is just as effective as an expensive one, buy the cheaper cleanser.

11. Aim for variety in your meals. Don't serve a dish of all meat one day and then next day a meal that is all vegetables. Aim for a mixture of foods in your meals.

12. Make lists of everything in the house. That way if you need something, but have forgotten where it is, you will know where to look. Keep these lists up to date.

13. Be careful about strangers calling. Always check their credentials before letting them into your house.

All right, it is simple, but it is only the beginning of the book and I like its plain workmanlike prose and the absence of superfluous adjectives. I can see that Dostoevsky was trying to say something about God, suffering and society, but I am not very clear what. Surely it would have been better if he had put his ideas down straightforwardly in numbered paragraphs, rather than trying to put these ideas all larded up in novels, where actresses, policemen, monks and whatnot spout them in a jumbled-up fashion? Anyway I have a shrewd suspicion that Baxter's ideas are more useful. I don't want to spend my days mooning about the house wondering if I am the world's greatest saint or sinner. The truth is that I am just ordinary.

Now I see that I have been a bit too successful with the breadcrumbs. The grease-mark has gone all right, but now that patch is much paler than the rest of the wallpaper. That is the trouble with trying to clean just a part of the wallpaper. It's turning chilly again. I really ought to put something on. Like many women I like doing the housework in the nude –

sometimes. I believe in taking risks in life, and working in the nude gives me a *frisson*. On the other hand, sometimes I like to be not only dressed for my housework but even overdressed. It's all a matter of mood, of impulse. That's the kind of creature I am – sometimes business-like, sometimes dreamy, sometimes larky, sometimes a little *triste*. Just because I am one person it does not mean that I have got only one personality.

So up I go to the bathroom. Mucor hisses welcomingly. Well, it's not much of a welcome; more threats. I pretend to pay it no attention and pick up the clothes I left lying about on the floor, and Mucor reverts to muttering to itself. It's a sort of witter really, but a sinister witter. Mucor is possessed by the idea that I have something that belongs to it and the Forces of Evil behind it – some little fleck of dirt, I gather. If someone wanted to hide a fleck of dirt, where would they hide it? In a desert? But Mucor has counted its way through the grains of sand in the Gobi and has not found it ... It must be in my house somewhere.

I am putting back on the clothes I was wearing for the coffee morning. I can't get interested in Mucor's lost little bit of dirt. As I say, I sometimes like to be overdressed for the housework. I am a bit of a heretic about this. I am not one of those Moping Monas who believe that one has to be drably dressed to do the cleaning. Putting on clothes is like putting on a performance I always think. Also I believe in sometimes aiming for what I think is known as an alienation effect. At the moment I am pulling on a white straight skirt, slightly more than knee length. There is a single-breasted jacket to go with it. It's dressing against type really – maybe that's why Rosemary and Stephanie kept looking at me this morning? The suit is quite tight and if I am to kneel down, to do some scrubbing say, the jacket will constrict my movements and the skirt is liable to ride up. This sort of thing has the effect of alienating me from my labour. I mean that it allows me to stand back, so to speak, and think about who I am and what is the nature of my work. It makes me more aware – like pretending to be a cripple doing the washing up.

Obviously I am quite fashion-conscious. I look at the fashion pages in *Cosmopolitan* when I can, and reading Roland Barthes's *Elements of Semiology* has been quite an eye-opener for me. It has made me see my dressing as operating within a code and setting up oppositions within that code. For instance the formality of the suit I am putting on is opposed to the free-ranging, open-ended nature of housework, and its whiteness is opposed to the dirt I am combating. Getting dressed is quite a consciousness-raising thing.

Well, now to finish the washing up and maybe fix myself some lunch, though it's really much too late for lunch already. Oh, but there's someone at the door!

CHAPTER
ELEVEN

The doorbell rings. I open the door and look out. The man on the steps looks poised and professional. He wears a three-piece suit and horn-rim glasses. He carries a white coat over his arm. I make the bold deductive leap:

'Hello. You must be from the Institute of Whiteness.'

That shakes his poise somewhat. He stands there considering, as if he were deciding who to be that day. He comes swiftly to the decision.

'Ermph. You were expecting me?'

'Well, not expecting, but I was hoping that you would call. How can I help you?'

'Perhaps it is rather a matter of what I can do for you. If I could come in and have a few words ...'

'Come in, then. Where would you like to see, the bathroom, the living room, the lavatory ...?'

'Wherever you feel most comfortable talking.'

He cocks his head and eyes me triumphantly. That beautifully judged reply has given him the ascendancy and made me uncomfortable. I don't like Dr Hornrim (for so I have mentally christened him), but still, an expert from the Institute of Whiteness! Can he be real? I let my eyes go out of focus, then focus again and he is still there. I am not going to allow myself to be rattled by him.

'Oh, in that case come up to the bathroom. That's where we keep the washing-machine. I expect that you would like to see the washing-machine.'

He looks dubious but follows me up anyway.

He stalks into the bathroom like a hunting panther. His eyes miss nothing – my toothbrush with the toothpaste still on it, the linen-basket piled high with unwashed clothes, a pair of tights dangling out of the washing-machine door – and there is Mucor clinging to the wall above the bath. Surely he does not miss Mucor? But he says nothing. Mucor whispers agitatedly to itself. I grab things from the linen-basket and shove them in until the machine is full (that means two thirds full; the machine won't work properly if it is jam-packed full). I am talking all the time while I do this, about coloureds, biological cleaners and the boil wash. It is the sense of his eyes boring into my back that makes me babble. But at last the machine is loaded, the door slammed shut, the dial turned. I pull myself together and turn to face him with my fingertips lightly resting on the machine which is beginning to throb. However I may feel, I am aware that I must seem confident and pretty, capable of handling the household wash.

His question comes like a karate chop:

'How do you feel about all this?'

'All this? Oh, you mean the wash. All right I suppose. Some things don't come out as well as others. The sweat in the armpits of Philip's shirts and understains ... understains are particularly difficult. It's because of the proteins in understains, I suppose.'

I forage about in the linen-basket, looking for something suitable to show him, but all the best bits have gone into the machine already. A brief hesitation and then I pull my skirt up and step out of my knickers. I hand them to him to look at. I can see that he is fascinated by the understain on the gusset. This is of course not the sort of thing I would do normally, but he is a man of science, professionally distanced from such intimacies.

Mucor, however, has been excited by the vision of an understain so very close to me and his hissing has become audible to me:

'For him or for me? You are the biodegradable woman, Marcia. The ultimate biodegradable woman. I'll hump you in pools of sweat and stains and pus. Pus, pus, pus.' Then, seeing that this is having no effect on me, Mucor changes tack. 'This is mad. Why do you have a man in your bathroom examining your knickers? It's all fantasy. This man is not real. He is a metaphor for the power of male science to intervene in the domestic domain of the female. Take a tip from me. You have got him excited now. Seduce him and get him down to the kitchen and take the bread-knife to him and see how easily he falls apart. He is not real, you know.'

'Did you hear what I said, Mrs ... Marcia? May I call you Marcia?' Dr Hornrim does not look excited, just impatient.

'Yes – er, no, I didn't hear what you said.'

'I said, is it that the washing and the housework are getting you down?'

'Well, sometimes. Who doesn't get the washday blues sometimes? But I know that perfect whiteness is not attainable yet. But that's what the Institute is working towards, isn't it?' I tilt my head and put my finger to my cheek in a gesture that I think is simultaneously intelligent and attractive. 'What I would like to know is how can the Institute help me?'

'You recognize that you need help?'

'Sure. What with the wash and the dishes and the hoovering, who doesn't?'

'Take the bread-knife to him, Marcia. You have the power. Human filth! Blood and guts all over the kitchen table!'

Mucor's exospore is rigid with excitement.

I am finding the hissing very distracting, and a nasty doubt is beginning to seep into my mind. If Hornrim is from the Institute, why is it that he hasn't registered the presence of Mucor? He looks quite old and competent, but I am wondering if he is Dr at all. He may just be some junior starting at the Institute with no research qualifications. Hornrim – maybe Dr Hornrim – takes off his glasses and rubs them very carefully. Curiously, without the lenses his eyes seem even more piercing.

'Marcia, would you say that you have many friends?'

'Not many, no.'

'But some?'

'Some, certainly. Why, only this morning we had a coffee morning downstairs. Eight or nine people came. Rosemary Crabbe the novelist was here.'

'But some would only be coffee morning acquaintances. Any special friends? People you feel that you could trust?'

'Well, there's Mrs Yeats. Possibly her.'

'Stephanie. Yes.'

What is all this? He seems more interested in me than my

whites. But I may have underestimated him. Suddenly he swoops back to the subject:

'Suppose, for example, I or someone else were to say to you that not only is your washing not perfectly white, but some other people get their clothes whiter than you do. Suppose that someone were to hint that there is an improved technique for getting things white, something that is a complete secret?'

'I would say that I would be interested to learn about this so-called improved technique.'

'That is a very positive attitude to take, Marcia. Most encouraging.'

'Kill him, Marcia.' Mucor's message is more urgent yet. 'Get him into the kitchen where the knives are. Now. I've worked it out. He is a real doctor and he thinks that you are mad. If you let him go, he will be back with a strait-jacket for you. Take him before he takes you. Just us is cosy.'

Ignoring Mucor's ravings I reach for a packet and tip a little of the soap powder into my hand. It rests quiet, white and still on my palm, its immense powers of lather quite latent. It is power within my grasp. I thrust it at him. I want him to take some of this deceptively quiet powder, but he still has my knickers in his hands and does not know where to put them, so my gesture remains unconsummated. I am going to show this man in a suit that he does not know it all. I am going to give him a taste of the discourse of detergent power, power to thrust and drive out, to lift off dirt; in the fight for family hygiene it kills germs – both known germs and unknown germs – and breaks down bacteria, it smashes, beats and bites. Soused with water, it combats dirt like a mad Lascar. The only language detergent power understands is violence. Together I and my powder, we conquer.

I start, 'In the fight against dirt –'

He cuts me short there.

'The fight against dirt? Can you tell me why your fight against dirt is important, Marcia?'

I am so irritated by his snotty questions that I come close to throwing the powder in his face. However I master myself with some difficulty.

'Because ... because I think ... take dust for example. No, let's start with thought. Do you know what the smallest unit of thought is? I don't, but it is certainly very small. We cannot possibly imagine how small our thoughts are. And when we have had them, they drift off and float around – '

'Like spores,' Mucor adds helpfully.

' – like spores and eventually they attach themselves to the hard grit cores of dust particles, and the dust and the thoughts mingle together in unswept places and then the thoughts begin to decay and the decay of thought is evil. The decay of reason produces monsters. Have I got it right so far?'

'You are most interesting. Go on.'

I take a deep breath, but then I hesitate. I start feeling a little clammy inside. I have noticed something, something that a delegate from the Institute of Whiteness really shouldn't have. A stain on his tie.

'By the way, do you know that you have got a stain on your tie?'

He looks casually down at it. 'I have, haven't I? You are very observant.'

'You can't put it in the washing-machine, you know.'

'I know. The colours tend to run. On the other hand, I would not trust a dry-cleaner's with a tie.'

I relax a little. Perhaps he is from the Institute after all. He seems to know the elementary stuff at least. Deep breath again.

'From the point of view of mental hygiene, the free association of discarded thoughts can be very dangerous. In a healthily functioning human brain there are billions of cells. It takes billions of particles of dust before the mental powers of dust can begin to match the powers of the human brain, but what some people don't realize is how easy it is for a billion dust particles to accumulate in the unswept corner of a room. They pile on top of one another, gathering dead thoughts. These dark brains interfere with ours and send messages to us. I'm healthy, thank God, and my house is fairly clean.'

'So you feel happy when you have got the house fairly clean?'

What is he getting at? He's asked something like that before. I clean the dirt. I drive it out of my house. And I am content.

What more should there be? It is like a doctor asking his houseman, 'Are you happy with your work – I mean just curing patients? Wouldn't you like to torture them a bit first?' Does Dr Hornrim – if that is his name – want me to torture dirt?

'What else should I do with a dirty house?'

He smiles thinly. He finds it amusing. I bloody well don't.

'I see that we are talking at cross purposes.' He runs his thumb against the hard edge of his jaw. 'Am I right in supposing that you suppose that I have come here to examine your washing-machine?'

The machine throbs beneath my fingertips. Who is teaching who? I wonder. It is Mucor he should examine. Mucor raves on,

'If he is not a doctor, he does not have a white coat. He does have a white coat and so he is a doctor. He will get you locked up. You do not know what confinement is like.'

Mucor has known what confinement is like. He can paint a grim picture of the nineteenth-century precursor of the Institute of Whiteness, La Savonnerie. The Savonnerie or Guild Temple of Balneotherapy, despite its French-sounding name, lay in the shadow of the dirt and cinder mounds at what is now King's Cross. In those days there were woods to the north of it and much of the labour employed was village labour. The folk were employed in hauling sleds of rubbish from the mounds into the Savonnerie itself. Dredger-men bring other types of rubbish up from the Regent's Canal. Just recently yet another kind of filth has been obtained from the skin of lunatics. This is an age when great strides have been made in the classification of dirt. Sir Francis Galton has published on the marks left by fingers, and Holmes's no less epoch-making *Seven Types of Tobacco Ash* is being eagerly read.

'Dust or Ugliness Redeemed' is written in letters of iron over the great gates of the Savonnerie. Beneath these words there is a ceaseless toing and froing, physicians and sewage engineers, stevedores and dredgermen, boilermen and charring ladies – and there are the distinguished visitors. Sir Francis Galton has been here of course, and his even more famous uncle Charles Darwin. So has Mrs Beeton. Today Charles

Dickens is to be shown round, and if Dickens should write favourably about the Savonnerie's work, who knows, perhaps the Prince Consort may come? Dickens's party are ushered first into the Superintendent's office. The Superintendent is effusive and gives them tea. The Superintendent keeps referring to himself by name in the hope of seeing that name in print in one of Dickens's articles. Dickens, vastly irritated, makes a mental note to forget it, and indeed it has been forgotten. After poring over a map of the works and being shown different types of dirt under glass slides, the party are conducted to the viewing gallery. This involves going out into the wintry air once more, for the viewing gallery is reached by an outside staircase that runs along the wall of the vast barn-like structure in which the main vats are tended. The Superintendent's deputy, a quieter man with a genuine enthusiasm for his work, leads them up the stairs. He takes the arm of the prettiest of the ladies. There is a lot of giggling among the party as they ascend. It conceals nerves. What horrors may they see inside?

Inside the long chamber their heads are more or less level with the rafters. The noise is enough to drive one out of one's mind. There is the clanking of chains and buckets coming up from the wells. There is the cranking of the gears that drive and turn the long wooden spoon-like objects that stir the mud in the vats. Rejected sludge gurgles as it trickles out of bung-holes at the bottom of the vats. And, more distantly outside the main chamber, there is the perpetual din of people shouting, doors slamming and keys turning. Here in the long gallery of the Savonnerie we are spectators at the beginning of the Great Incarceration of Dirt. These pioneering reformers are going to have it shut up in bags, bins and sewage tanks. The deputy has to cup his hands and shout to make himself heard. When he is heard one of the great wooden spoons is made to rise from a vat up almost to the level of the horrified gaze of the visitors; wrapped around the ladle-end is a woman's soiled shift.

Down goes the spoon again into the central mudbath. Attendants recommence their experiments, squirting jets of water into the vat and running electric currents through the water.

The men tend to the vats and the electric batteries. The women, heavily muscled launderesses, keep clear of the danger area and are employed in the grating of large cakes of soap. Meanwhile Dickens is warming to the deputy. He finds the young man's attentions extremely flattering. Why, the deputy claims to have been put on the road to his present career by reading *Great Expectations*! That scene with Miss Havisham and the dusty bridal feast!

'I tell you I know key passages by heart and can recite it from memory,' shouts the deputy. And he does so:

' "... was spacious, and I dare say had once been handsome, but every discernible thing in it was covered with dust and mould, and dropping to pieces. The most prominent object was a long table with a table-cloth spread on it, as if a feast had been in preparation when the house and the clocks all stopped together. An épergne or centre-piece of some kind was in the middle of this cloth; it was so heavily overhung with cobwebs that its form was quite indistinguishable; and, as I looked along the yellow expanse out of which I remember its seeming to grow, like a black fungus, I saw speckled-legged spiders with blotchy bodies running home to it, and running out from it, as if some circumstance of the greatest public importance had just transpired ..." '

The deputy could have continued, but he is interrupted by the Superintendent.

'The Devil's supper!' quips the Superintendent, pointing at the long spoons rotating in the vats. No one laughs, and the Superintendent moves on to tell Dickens all about his wife and his lovable brood of infants.

Dickens loses interest in the talk. He gazes down at the turbid shapes being stirred in the mud, seeing in them images of insanity, poverty and crime. He is working presently on the ending of *Edwin Drood*. It has become necessary for the Superintendent to rejoin the party now, for his presence is obligatory before the latest technique for extracting filth can be demonstrated. He makes signals, and two of the launderesses move to open the large wooden double door at the end of the chamber. Through the doors the visitors can see a smaller room, well lit by gas. In the centre of the room is a leather armchair. Strapped to the armchair is a lunatic. The director claps his hands, and jets of water spray down on the lunatic. Everybody laughs. The lunatic squirms. Sluice channels carry his filth and urine down to a small experimental vat in the main chamber. The filth will mix with water. Then the water will be boiled off and we shall have the distilled essence of madness and fear.

The lunatic has his eyes shut and is dazedly trying to shake his head away from the water. Behind his shaking head a dark patch can be detected on the leather chair-back. It is not the first time that this chair has been used for this experiment and the leather has suffered somewhat. The dark shape on the chair-back is the black exospore of common household mould, Mucor. Mucor is sending dark thoughts to the famous author in the gallery, in demented determination to secure for household mould a central role in the ending of *Edwin Drood*. Perhaps he will be successful. Dickens's mind is turning over ...

The Superintendent claps his hands again, and the two launderesses struggle to close the doors. The one on the left, Nelly, has a husband, Valentine. Valentine does not work in the Savonnerie, but he has secured for himself a place in a ships' chandler's in the Docks area. While Dickens (and Mucor) work on the ending of *Edwin Drood*, Nelly is thinking about what she will do when the day's work is over. She and Valentine will take the train to Denmark Hill (LBSCR) and visit the Lava Rink. Friday night is roller-skating night for Valentine and Nelly. The management have just acquired the new Plimpton skates with rubber pads which give assistance in changing the direction of the (wooden) wheels. Nelly also likes to flirt with the skateboy while she is having her skates strapped on. But for now she can only dream of the night's giddy pleasures when she will step out with Valentine.

'All mad, you know,' Mucor addresses me directly. 'With the best of intentions, but little serious thought, the people at the Savonnerie were stumbling in a sort of half-witted way towards what they hoped would be the washing-machine. All hopelessly misconceived. Evil simply fermented in those huge unsterilized vats. The real technical ancestry of the washing-machine turned out to be quite different. And yet, and yet it was a precursor, the precursor of the Institute of Whiteness, and, when you think of it, is this trivial thing of tin that whirrs and throbs in the corner of your bathroom really worthy of the name of "washing-machine"? I think not. But you are. You are the real machine that washes in this house. You are the mechanical bride. Darwin, Dickens, Beeton – if the Victorians ever invented anything, it is you.'

Dirt under torture is not a pretty sight. Because of this, or perhaps because of the stench, one of the ladies in the gallery has been seized by spasms of vomiting. The front of her dress, which is of silk, is covered with vomit.

'How do you get vomit stains out of silk?'

If I were to go for Hornrim with a kitchen knife, it would be hard to take him unawares. Even now, when he is bemused by my question, he retains a combative panther-like alertness.

'I don't know. But the tie is not silk and the stain is not vomit.'

He snatches his glasses from his face, snaps them shut and puts them in a case in his pocket.

'I think my visit has been most useful. Perhaps you would be good enough to show me out?'

Reluctantly I lead him downstairs. I was not expecting him to go so suddenly. I am confused and suspicious.

'Wouldn't you like to come into the kitchen? I could make some tea, and there are still some things I would like you to put my mind at rest about.' (Household stains, the problem of evil, Hornrim's own credentials from the Institute of Whiteness.)

But he moves ahead of me and hurries to the door.

Mucor hisses underfoot, as if in agony, 'Don't let him go, Marcia! If you do he will be back soon with a strait-jacket.'

'I will be back soon,' says Hornrim. 'Goodbye, Marcia.'

'Goodbye, Dr Hornrim,' I cry.

He smiles faintly. 'Doctor, anyway,' and he is gone.

Mucor does not think that we shall be alone together for very long.

CHAPTER
TWELVE

Why am I not a Brillo pad? Or the bit of gunge at the bottom of the pan that I am using the Brillo on now? I might have been a Brillo pad or not existed at all. It all seems so arbitrary, this assignment of who I am. There is only one 'Marcia' in the world and the chances of *my* being the same as that 'Marcia' seem infinitely small – particularly when I consider the number of Brillo pads there are lying around, perhaps waiting to take my identity. Of course, as a Brillo pad I would not have self-consciousness. That is irrelevant. I would unconsciously exist as an unselfconscious Brillo pad. To be this hard-working, chemically treated mesh-work of wire!

Experimentally I declaim to the empty kitchen, 'I am a Brillo pad!'

There is a sudden rustling behind me. It is the sort of sound which, at the instant you hear it, makes you go cold all over. You fancy a rat dropping on to the meat in the larder or something worse. Then you realize that it is a piece of paper that has been lying in awkward tense folds on the kitchen table all day and has arbitrarily chosen that precise moment to re-arrange its folds and rest in new crumples that are more in conformity with the force of gravity. I spin round. Where I should have seen a piece of crumpled paper I find myself staring at a grinning face.

'You are a Brillo pad. You are the dirt at the bottom of the pan – or, as the Hindus would have it, "Thou art the bowman and the bow. Thou art the slayer and the slain. Therefore Arjuna draw thy bow and fear not!" But I am surprised to hear the doctrines of the Bhagavad-Gita falling from your lips, Marcia.'

'Oh, Teilhard! Is that you? Then it must be tea time.'

He nods and smiles. Flustered, I rattle on, 'Oh, I do feel a fool, fancying myself a Brillo pad and talking to myself. I didn't realize you were here. I thought you were still in the

Gobi. How was the Gobi? Did you bring the dig to a successful conclusion? Can you help me with the tea things?'

'No need to be embarrassed. No need at all. A Brillo pad is perfectly good to think with. Professional philosophers often take their examples from the mundane and the familiar ...' He stands lost in thought. He is not making a move to help me with the tea things. 'They say that they do this to make their problems easier to understand, but I sometimes wonder if their aim is not rather to make the familiar seem strange to us. The expedition was a wash-out, by the way. We lost everything in the storms. Even before the dust began to rise, Mucor was at work. You must remember. Oh, how we missed you, Marcia! The Mongols are an admirable people but they are not famous for their washing up. I confess that I found tea with scones in the Gobi something of an ordeal. You must picture it. It is summer. In the summer the Bactrians are in full moult and very irritable from skin sores. The fire is being got ready and the second cameleer is melting a great pat of camel-dung into the fire to get it going. Once it is going, he returns to kneading the dough for the scones. No washing of hands, for he estimates that the fire purifies all things. Meanwhile the first cameleer has been picking the scabs off the Bactrians. Now he returns and scoops his hand in the butter and off he goes to smooth the butter into the camels' open sores. No washing of the hands for him either. Then back he comes and, when the scones are ready, the two cameleers spread the butter on the scones with their fingers. Oh, how much I prefer your English teas! I need not say that, before it was time for the rising of the Great Winds, half the expedition was laid low with food poisoning.'

Now I am ready to move off with a tray-load of stuff into the living room. Teilhard follows me, talking all the time.

'Then when the Great Winds blew up we had no strength to resist and the sands covered what we had uncovered. I was bitter of course. I freely confess it to you. I wept. But as I stood watching the yellow clouds whipping over my work, a great peace came upon me. What was I doing in the Gobi? How had I thought that I should find some great Truth in this oriental wasteland? Was it not my running away? As the poet

Novalis says, "Where are we really going? Always home!" So I have returned. And, you know, science is not enough. There must be the spirit too. As I stood looking on the dust storms and listening to the mockery of Mucor in the howling of the wind, the words of Blake came to me:

> The Atoms of Democritus
> And Newton's Particles of light
> Are sands upon the Red Sea shore
> Where Israel's tents do shine so bright.

'Do you know Blake, Marcia?'

'I know Blake. Hello, William.'

Blake nods affably to show that we are indeed well acquainted with one another. Squeezed in with Blake on the sofa are Leonardo and Dickens. The two chairs by the window have been taken by Charles Darwin and his talented nephew Sir Francis Galton. (That's a surprise! I shall need more cups.) De Hooch has perched himself as far away from Blake as he can get. Teilhard, finding nowhere else to sit, descends to a cross-legged position on the floor.

I introduce those who do not already know one another. I am feeling for once a bit one up on Teilhard, who is gazing in awe at Blake, Leonardo and Dickens. To do him credit, though, he is honest about it.

'When one is young, one thinks to oneself that when one shall have been acknowledged a genius, there shall be the end of it. But here in your living room, Marcia, I am conscious that I am only at the foothills of genius. A relative nobody in the pantheon of geniuses. My mind has really more in common with yours, than with theirs, Marcia. Let us hope that they will speak slowly so that we can understand. To be a third-class genius . . . it is not a pleasant feeling.'

I smile sympathetically.

'Well, that's all the introductions done. I think that we are going to need another pot and some more cakes. Would anyone like to come and help me in the kitchen?'

They all look shiftily at one another. All these geniuses and not one of them knows how to make a pot of tea! So out I go on my own. When I come back I find Darwin examining the cake that is already on the table. It has a little bit of mould on one of its edges.

'My dear, your cake has acquired an entrancing cryptogamic fungus. I last had just such a mould on cake when we were at anchor off Tierra del Fuego. How singular is the relationship between parasitical moulds and the cakes on which they grow in distant parts of the world!'

He assures me that it is quite harmless to eat, but I recognize the mould for what it is, a focus for the thoughts and words of Mucor. Dickens meanwhile is engaged in telling Galton how he has recently been inspired to conceive of the ending for *Edwin Drood*.

'Ooh, I hope you are not going to put me in it!' exclaims Galton. No, he is not.

This is what we hear:

'... Will you not join us in a game of cards?' Trapman's manner of address towards the prisoner is polite and even ceremonious.

When Necker sees that the prisoner makes no response, he laughs and calls to his fellow gaoler, 'Deal out the cards for the two of us then, Mr Trapman! Soon enough the Governor will give this fellow 'is deal suit.'

'His deal suit, Mr Necker?'

''is eternity box, Mr Trapman.'

'His coffin, Mr Necker?'

'That's it, Mr Trapman. A fine rope cravat for the singing master!'

(It must be owned that the excess of Necker's ill-will towards the prisoner fully makes up for any excess of civility on the part of Trapman towards the same.)

'Double demon, Mr Necker?'

'That's the very ticket, Mr Trapman! Deal out the cards and leave the prisoner to 'is vittles.'

John Jasper – for it is he – pays his gaolers no heed. It has been well said that when a man knows that he is to be hanged in the morning it concentrates his mind wonderfully. Jasper does not hear the slap of the cards on the table, for all his faculties are engrossed in the contemplation of a stale and musty hunk of bread that is in his hand. See, as he gazes, at what he gazes! A ring of mould has extended itself over a goodly part of the bread's exterior. A man more optimistically disposed might compare its circle to a fairy ring encountered in the woods, but Jasper's morbid condition leads him to fancies that have nothing of the fairy in them.

As he gazes shall he not see the noose and the twisting of its braids and the looping of the knot and the tightening of its knot? The hitching of the knot of death might lead him on to call to memory how he had once schemed to hitch the knot of happiness with the lovely young orphan, Miss Rosa Budd, and had dreamed of pressing the ring of wedlock on her finger. Other memories come unbidden. A napkin ring is the same shape as a wedding ring, but its significance is quite different. There was a napkin ring that rolled across the table when he, Jasper, sprang up to attack and chloroform young Edwin Drood, his own ward and, as he believed, the fiancé of that same Miss Budd. Such queer and fantastical rings! How can a wedding ring revolve into a napkin ring and the napkin ring distend itself into a noose? Very simply; such transformations are commonplace in the thousand false dawns of the opium den. It was in such a den in Limehouse – Jack Chinaman its proprietor – that Jasper has the young Edwin secreted and confined. The deranged choirmaster feeds his young ward opium and seeks to make him sing like a canary in a cage. The den is squalid, the brass opium-pipes are tarnished, and the mesmeric eyes of Mr John Jasper are the only things that glitter in the den's obscurity. Hypnotism and drugs bind Edwin fast – as surely as if he had been pitched into a well. Unhappy Drood shall be forced to renounce Miss Budd and much else besides.

Surely he must see the smoke rings ascending from the pipes of the drugged? (The smoke rings are of a yellowish brown, the colour of ivory that has been left in shadow.) Surely he must see where such a ring must end? The opium smoker sees and forgets. The rings darken. Jasper has learnt from the lips of Miss Budd that all his labours have been in vain. Moreover the suspicions of 'Princess Puffer' have been aroused by the activities in the den of her neighbour and rival, Jack Chinaman. Drood must be done away with and speedily. Jasper's scarf encircles Drood's neck. Its circle tightens. That was swiftly done, but there is the body to be disposed of too.

Round and round the rings are turning. Jasper hits on the notion of conveying the cadaver to the quicklime pits at King's Cross, just outside the walls of La Savonnerie. A muscular launderess, hurrying for her train, glimpses two men with sacks talking beside the quicklime pits. That there are two men who so stand with their sacks conversing quietly in the darkening light is a matter of considerable indifference to her and she walks on in the direction of her train, but to one of the men in question, John Jasper – for it is he – this same conference gives rise to the most lively fears. Unhappy mischance that his acquaintance, Durdles, has chosen this evening of all evenings to come up with a sack of Cloisterham grave-dust to sell to La Savonnerie! (But here, reader, there is no fiction; this vile trade in morbid rubbish is openly espoused by philanthropists and such-like folk in the name of science and hygiene and God knows what.) At length Durdles shuffles off and Jasper is able to tip his own deathly load into a quicklime pit. As the sack sinks beneath the surface, it creates eddies and the eddies in turn arrange themselves in a spiralling vortex (counter-clockwise). Ah, must he not see this?

It is just this sort of movement of random turbulence that Jasper was to recall and compare in his mind with the sensation he created a week later when he burst in upon the circle of 'geniuses' that had gathered to read tragedies with the solicitor's assistant, Bazzard – for comparisons are always possible when there is a movement of a considerable quantity of something, whether it be of water or of genius. In that same swirling instant when Jasper identified Bazzard with Datchery, the mysterious spy at Cloisterham, Bazzard rose to his feet, pointed to Jasper and turning to his circle of 'geniuses' cried, 'There, gentlemen, is the murderer of Edwin Drood!' The hunt is on, first in London, then in Cloisterham. The flashing circle, the gleaming lens of Mr Tartar's telescope, falls on the fugitive

Jasper in Cloisterham Cathedral Close, like the avenging eye of God, and this glittering circle does indeed signal the apprehension of the homicidal choirmaster of Cloisterham.

A circle, a lens, a noose, a passage out of this world. He would escape these sickly fancies, but everywhere his vision is circumscribed. It is as if Jasper's hypnotic gaze has been turned inwards to gaze at the abyss of his soul. Round and round. Up come images of poverty, crime and insanity, like bubbles rising to form a scum. There can be no end to these meditations. What ring of power can have provoked them? But see! It is only a ring of mould on a crust of bread being chewed by a condemned man on the last of that man's false dawns.

Dickens has been talking at full gallop. He has held us all enthralled. Abruptly now he collapses on to the sofa mopping his brow.

'Jolly good, Charlie!'

'Such shadows – and such light!'

After a few more such appreciative murmurs nobody knows what to say, and there is a busy reaching for cups and cakes. Finally Darwin turns to regard Leonardo's noble profile. Conscious of being watched, Leonardo is impelled to return his gaze and wait for him to speak. At last Darwin does so:

'Do you like scones?'

'Very much,' and Leonardo, his mind at ease again, resumes his munching of one.

More silence. I can see that I will have to get the party going.

'This reminds me of this morning. I was hostess to a coffee morning in this room. Actually, although it's afternoon –'

'Late afternoon,' interrupts Blake. (I can see that he is worrying about me, worrying what will happen when Philip comes home.)

' – although it's afternoon, this could be a sort of coffee morning. We could have one.'

'What is a coffee morning?' asks De Hooch.

'Oh well ... you have a few friends round and you just sit around and talk about things. I am your hostess.'

'A *causerie* then,' says Dickens.

'A symposium,' offers Leonardo.

'What sort of things are we supposed to talk about?' Teilhard wants to know. I can see that he is worried whether he is going to be able to keep his end up.

'Well, sometimes we talk about our houses and cars and our children ...'

'We have no children,' several of the geniuses mutter.

I rush on: 'But more often, my friends and I, we like to talk about art and literature and religion, plays we have seen and issues like the politics of sexism. It takes us out of ourselves. I thought that with all you lot here we might talk about something like "The Responsibility of the Artist in Society", or perhaps "The Two Cultures" – you know, whether art and science are compatible.' I look brightly round.

'Excuse me. That is very dull,' opines De Hooch. There is general agreement.

'Dear lady, I confess that hitherto I have never found the leisure to consider such topics, worthy of consideration though they certainly are.' Having said this, Darwin carefully cuts a slice off the cake, selecting the bit which has the mould on it, and he starts talking to himself – or is it to the mould?

I look imploringly at Dickens. He sits a little more erectly and then once more he is in full flight:

'Gentlemen, dear friends and mine hostess – and particularly my hostess, who has challenged us to address ourselves to the topic of the Artist in Society – in responding to her call – and I am honoured to find myself among those to whom that call was addressed – I find that I stand in some awe of the immense largeness of the topic. A resonant topic, yes! The Artist! His Society! His Responsibilities! Vast and chilly phrases. Cold abstractions. The Artist does not need to eat nor scratch his itch. He does not lie awake in his restless bed troubled by the fear that he may have forgotten to put the cat out and that that cat in the darkest fall of night, in the extremity of its need, may be defiling the kitchen floor. But *an* artist does. One such as our friend here!' (Pointing at De Hooch.) 'A man of flesh and blood, no cold abstraction, he has known the laughing joys of infant perceptions and the sorrows of a maturer age – child and man, as are we all.'

Dickens pauses and looks round before resuming:

'Yet what is an artist – or, more generally, a genius – without some woman to care for him? Some woman, it may be his wife, or his housekeeper or perhaps his motherless daughter (pity her plight!), she laughs and weeps with the genius. Yes! But she does not only stand aside in life's fray, laughing and weeping away. No! She washes his shirts and she sweeps away the rejected products of his genius that lie discarded around his feet, the ill conceived drafts, the hasty sketches, broken pencil-stubs. She is the handmaid of genius – but this is too general. I will be precise. Such a one is Marcia! God bless you, Marcia!'

There is a ragged toast of teacups.

'Your husband must be a remarkable man.'

Galton's question (it is really a question) catches me by surprise.

'Philip? Oh no, he's just ordinary.'

'A very remarkable man, as I am sure we shall find.'

'Oh no, you will all be gone by the time he gets back.'

Dickens shakes his head smiling:

'Well, we shall see.' Then, abruptly, 'And if I again hesitate in trepidation when I am asked to broach the theme of the Two Cultures –'

'Excuse me, please,' interrupts De Hooch. 'There are not two cultures but three. There is art culture, science culture and germ culture. The first two should be allies against the third.'

'Just so. And, besides, the vastness of the topic confounds our apprehensions –'

'Fuels our apprehensions, you mean.' This is Blake.

'I meant that it confuses our understanding, though certainly it increases my fear also. I shall now give shape and colour to my fear.' Dickens looks wildly round at his audience. He seems uncertain how to proceed, yet proceed he does:

'Gentlemen, I want you to picture a carpet. Let it be a carpet of mystery, for its thick pile is the repository of secrets which are not the less curious for being little ones and they and it are darkened over in enigmatic half-shades. Picture a carpet that is neglected, save by one person who cares for it as best she knows how. If a man were then to be seen crawling over that carpet, a curious observer – one whom chance has brought to this scene – might muse to himself as he looked down at the man on hands and knees on the carpet, and his musings, very likely, would be as follows, "Hulloa! I do believe this man is drunk – but no! Confound it! There is too much system in the fellow's progress over the carpet! Here is a puzzle indeed!" But there is no such observer and no man crawls over that carpet, which still retains its mysteries. Yet if a man were to crawl over that carpet, he might make conjecture to himself. Aye! What might he not conjecture –'

'What not indeed! This is not up to your usual standard, Charlie. Where is this all leading to?' This is Galton.

'How may I picture this carpet, when you have revealed none of its lineaments?' Blake is equally peevish.

Dickens is almost feverish in his agitation. He pushes back a lock of hair and mops his brow again.

'Who was it who said, "Genius is nine tenths perspiration and one tenth inspiration"?' That was Teilhard. No, it was not Teilhard who said it, but it was Teilhard who said, 'Who was it who said ...' and so on, if you see what I mean. He is always saying things like that. A great quoter.

Suddenly Dickens is on his feet. His eyes seem to be on the verge of bursting from his skull. One arm sweeps out. The other points down to his feet.

'Gentlemen! Blind fools! I only know that the carpet – this carpet of mystery – is in this house and that I am standing on it at this very moment, and, if I have refrained from the description of its precise lineaments, I tell you that it is only because she who cares for it is in this same room and she is certainly a wiser guide to its mysteries than I could ever hope to be. Behold the woman! Marcia, please – ?'

Now I am in my element. This is very much my territory. The living-room carpet is not at all the same sort of carpet as that frayed thing in the hallway where Mucor has his headquarters. This is fawn-coloured Axminster in quite good nick.

Since I share Dickens's aversion to generalities, I am not going to lecture on the whole carpet, just a selected patch. I have devoted quite a lot of thought to this strangely neglected patch. I am down on the carpet encircling the patch in my arms.

If the hall carpet was all jungle and lagoons, this one is more savannah or pampas. There are no bare patches to remind us of the furrowed dead sea in the hallway. I am dealing with an area of, I suppose, some one hundred and twenty knots, plus a few outlying colonies of two or three knots that are congealed in darkness. We won't be looking at the knots themselves in any detail. I simply ask them to observe that the individual knot exists as a twisting column of fine-spun threads. I have remarked that the carpet's colour is fawn, but here at the level of local colour, the threads can be seen to give off a, perhaps illusory, golden shimmer. There are about one hundred and eighty such threads to each knot – that is an average. These threads go upwards twisting round upon themselves, like a multiple helix, or like barley-sugar, to take a more homely analogy. Each thread is tipped with blackness at the top. It is these little black tips which multiplied many thousands of times over and taken *en masse* give a general effect of grubbiness to the carpet.

By now I have really got them. Their tea things are forgotten, and all the geniuses are down on their knees beside me on the carpet. Addressing Leonardo particularly, I point out how the close packed knots incline in ripple patterns, like a still shot of a wind-tossed cornfield or eddying water. If we could just seize the meaning of these patterns ... But this greater mystery is (alas!) only the background to my own more restricted area of investigation, the dirt which mingles in with or lies over these carpet knots, the dirt which, in my eyes, forms the figure in the carpet and furnishes me with the point of my narration. The darkened tips of the knots I have already alluded to. They are trivial. But see here! The leaves and a few other smaller organic fragments which have drifted in through the window. And see there, picking its way along the narrow crevice between two rows of knots, that is a carpet-grub in its larval stage. It is commonly known as the woolly bear. Despite its rather cuddly name, the woolly bear is a destroyer. There is only one here, thank goodness. Let us follow its path and see where it is going. Yes, at the end of the crevice a dense cluster of knots has been fused together by a thick black substance which I take to be machine oil with some ground-in grit. It rises like a temple of evil in the faintly darkening plain.

The geniuses are only too fascinated by this structure. Such fascination can be dangerous. Let us pull back a little.

'So, sirs, we see that the general effect of dirtiness has been built up in layers, as if it were the creation of an artist's palette.' (What follows is for De Hooch's benefit.) 'The natural colour of the fabric threads has as it were been primed with artificial dyestuff, then lightly pounced with a dusting of grubbiness, but here and here we have the thick impasto of machine oil, and then a final glittering sheen of close ground grit to give surface texture, and all this ingenuity, these fine gradations of shadow, simply to create a dark figure on the carpet – and this figure is itself one of the least spectacular of the effects of the Empire of Mucor. I think that is as far as I can take you by way of a general introduction, though I am of course ready to answer questions on particular points of detail.'

There are murmurs of demurral. A few of the geniuses reach back for their cups of tea, which have grown cold in the meantime. Galton speaks:

'That was masterly, Marcia. The presentation of your vision was remarkable for its control. I was particularly intrigued by your identification of the temple of evil. I wonder if you would like to say a few words about that?'

'Yes. I see the temple as a forward colony of Mucor's, engaged in the propagation of evil in my living room. As to its actual identification – well, I think that reading patterns in the dirt is a skill that many people have. It is a skill which demands first and foremost humility. The skilled critic of dirt will indeed come to realize that she or he may be not so much reading it as writing it. I mean that to a certain extent she may be imposing her perceptions on the mess. The example I like to give is Hamlet with his cloud which was "very like a whale", where the uncertainty of his reading is, I believe, a product of his characteristic introspective humility.'

Now Blake raises his hand. 'The Dark Temple is closed to my senses five and where the woolly bear treads I dare not follow. Enchanted Atoms mock us from the Temple's columns. What is to be done? Angel, I see you weeping. How may we help?'

'I don't want to enter the temple. I want to destroy it. It gives off a negative emotional tonality –'

The writers in the group all wince.

'I'm sorry. You'll have to forgive this housewife, but you know what I mean. It gives off vibrations' (more wincing, but I press on) 'which are poisoning my relation with Philip. He hasn't commented on this particular patch of dirt or any other, but they are bound to have a sort of subliminal effect.' (Wincing again. Hell!) 'Anyway, machine oil with grit is very hard to get off from fabric like this. A Hoover is useless. I've tried shampoo. I have even tried bleach.'

I have been doing far too much talking. I think I have said enough to get them going. I ought to stop.

Teilhard is first with a suggestion:

'Can Philip not help you with this problem?'

'I thought you knew. My husband has no idea at all that all this is going on. It is your help I want.'

Darwin is the one I have pinned my hopes on. He is now subjecting the dirt to minute examination, while talking to Leonardo. De Hooch unhelpfully pours a little tea on the patch of carpet and silently contemplates the difference that this makes, but Galton and Teilhard soon join in the discussion. In a matter of minutes a brainstorming session is going on. I try to follow it, but the geniuses are talking very fast. The gist of what I have understood, mostly from Darwin, is as follows:

Classification is the key to the problem. Dirt has been mis-classified. To understand what is involved in classification a homely analogy might help. Classification is like tidying up. It is putting the right things in the right boxes. It is what I do when I scurry about the house putting the cushions back on the sofa and plumping them up, putting newspapers in the newspaper rack and so on. So every object in the house gets classified. There are classes of living-room objects, kitchen objects and so on. The order of things is just as important in housekeeping as it is in semantics, and a very untidy house may look like gibberish to another person. A thing is the sign of itself, but it is also a unit in the larger unit of communication, the room. There is also likely to be dirt in the room (philosophers' rooms are no exception here).

Dirt is a shorthand term for an anomalous class of objects which are perceived as interfering with the room's communication, and, in fact, the dirt is not communicating with us in the same way as the orderly array of objects on the mantelpiece, say. That its failure to communicate has come to be seen by thinkers like Leonardo and Darwin as a major problem in Western thought is due partly to a too anthropocentric classification of the types of dirt, and to the use of an unjustifiably affective vocabulary. For example 'thought-provoking dirt' or 'fear-provoking dirt' and simply and most commonly 'depressing dirt'. More profoundly however our problem is due to an insufficiently dynamic definition of dirt, for, yes, dirt has its own concealed dynamic. A breakthrough here will be achieved by totally transforming the frame of reference. It is not really so much by observation and experiment, but more by a shift in paradigms that the epistemological leap will take –

I cannot control my impatience any longer:

'Look, I will go nuts if by the time Philip gets home this oil stain is still on the floor. How is all this shifting of paradigms going to help?'

Darwin levelly returns my gaze, but he does not respond to its urgency.

'Directly ... not at all. But we have made great strides already. A transformation of thought is not achieved overnight or even necessarily within a century. I now regret not having even hinted at the problems in *The Origin of Species*. We here feel that dirt's concealed direction of movement is towards structures that are progressively (or as I prefer, regressively) more complex but less functional.'

He pats me on the shoulder. 'This is difficult for you, Marcia, I know –'

'It's not getting my carpet clean.'

'But it is difficult for me too. I am having to think in terms of a new sort of Gresham's Law where rubbish is driving out things that we regard as sensible – in terms of the continued survival and regressive development of the unfit. An analogy might help.'

'Like a wave that is simple in its form as it rises, but which, as it falls, breaks into fragments ... which the artist, try as he may ...' Leonardo's contribution tails off vaguely.

'What you are saying is like cornflakes' (this is my attempt to find a suitable scientific model) 'where the big unbroken bits stay on top, but the broken flakes as they get smaller drift down to the bottom of the pack.'

Darwin is suspicious, but Teilhard backs me up. Darwin and Leonardo would like to see these cornflakes. I add that in the case of tinned tomato juice on the other hand the thick stuff stays on top, while the thin stuff goes down to the bottom. Yes they would like to see that too. So back I go into the kitchen. I have to break into a new packet of cornflakes to find unbroken flakes. While I am still in the kitchen, the phone rings. So I go to the phone clutching my cornflakes and tomato juice.

'Marcia?'

'Yes, Philip?'

'Just ringing to say that I haven't got much on at the office today and I will be back early.'

'How soon?'

'Depends on the traffic. Twenty minutes or half an hour maybe.'

Further down the hallway the patch of mould that is Mucor is watching me with its solitary putrefied eye. It has said nothing since we started tea. It is biding its time. I am thinking that I am going to need a glass and a tin-opener for the tomato juice.

'Marcia, are you all right?'

'Yes, I'm fine. I was just thinking that I haven't got anything out of the freezer for us to eat tonight.'

'It doesn't matter about the food. Don't worry about that. Darling, when I get home, I think that there are some things we should talk about.'

Now De Hooch has started calling to me from the living room. He wants me to bring him two eggs – one boiled and one raw. He is an impatient man.

'OK. We'll talk when you get back. 'Bye, Philip.' I put the phone down and I go back into the kitchen and start putting things on the tray, while the egg is boiling. I wonder why Philip didn't ask about the coffee morning. There is quite a lot of noise coming from the living room now, muffled thumps and chuckles.

'Hurry up, Marcia. We need you.'

By the time I get back into the living room, things have quietened down. Most of the geniuses are back on their chairs, and Teilhard and Darwin are having a fairly serious argument about whether dirt and its devolution are part of the Divine Plan. Darwin says no; Teilhard says yes. However elsewhere in the room there is an atmosphere of suppressed merriment. The geniuses are relaxed and Leonardo, vigorously backed up by Blake and De Hooch, politely suggests that I take my clothes off and unbend a bit.

'I've got quite enough to worry about with this carpet, thank you.'

Darwin takes the cornflakes and having torn the cardboard box apart he starts shaking the inner packet about to show the stochastic patterns in the random descent of little flakes to the bottom. But, apart from Teilhard, everybody else is interested in what is going to be done with the eggs. The eggs were really for Leonardo, but being a bit shy, he got De Hooch to shout for them.

Leonardo takes the two eggs and sets them on their sides on the table and then he makes them spin. The two eggs spin out of phase with one another, and we can all see that the boiled egg (a soft-boiled three-minute egg) is spinning more slowly than the raw egg, and soon the boiled egg ceases to spin while the raw one continues to rotate slowly for quite a while longer.

'Here, sirs,' says Leonardo, 'we see the vortex of life. The raw egg still moves, but the cooked egg has had its livingness boiled out of it.'

'With respect, that is nonsense!' cries young Galton. 'What you have there is only an application of the principle of moments as it applies to fluids and to solids. Watch again!'

He grabs the two eggs and makes them spin. Unfortunately ... unfortunately he does it rather wildly and the raw egg spins off the table and smashes on the carpet. There are already a few cornflakes there, for in the meantime Darwin's bag has split open. I am about to tear a strip off them all, but at this point two things happen. The phone starts ringing again and De Hooch keels over on to the floor. Well! At first I think that the excitement with the eggs must have been too much for him and he has simply fainted. But do you groan so terribly before you faint? He lies very still on the floor. I think that he must be dead. The phone keeps ringing. Was this all too much for his great heart? Or has he poisoned himself with a bit of Darwin's mouldy cake? Seeing the consternation on my face, the other geniuses are convulsed with mirth. At last Teilhard lets me out of my misery:

'Killer Wink. Do you know Killer Wink, Marcia? The taxonomy of dirt and the reconceptualization of decayed thought-patterns, they are big problems, yes, but with the power of our combined minds the preliminary answers at least come fairly easy. So it is boring for us, no? So we decide while you were out in the kitchen, that we will play Killer Wink to amuse ourselves while we continue to advance towards the solution of these problems.'

I wish that bloody phone would stop ringing. Teilhard goes on to explain about Killer Wink. His voice seems to blend in with the ringing of the phone, high and insistent. Dickens had actually wanted to play Are You There, Moriarty?, a rather jovial game where two people lie on the floor beside one another, blindfolded, holding the partner's hand with one hand and clutching a rolled-up newspaper in the other. Then one calls out, 'Are you there, Moriarty?' and the other tries to swat him over the head with his rolled-up newspaper. However, the two baldies in the group, Leonardo and Darwin, vetoed this.

So they settled on the less disruptive Killer Wink. In Killer Wink secret lots are drawn to determine who is going to be the Killer. Then, while all the normal chat is going on the Killer strikes at his victims by surreptitiously winking at them. The victim is then honour-bound to collapse and expire with realistic groans, and, in doing so, not to make it obvious who it is who has winked at them. The rest of the group, a diminishing group, try to detect the winker.

I listen to all this with some incredulity. Teilhard stops talking and the phone stops ringing at the same time, and I start laying into them:

'The power of your combined minds for whom no problem is too great – or too small! All that I can see you have achieved so far is an almighty mess on my carpet. Don't bother to tell me what you want the tomato juice for as well. Solving problems and playing games serenely above it all while your handmaid bustles about you cleaning up! Three thousand years of art and science, of electron telescopes, elegies, cantilever bridges and frescoes, but is the lot of the common housewife any easier than it was three thousand years ago? I am speaking about almost half the world's population.'

'Science has given you the Hoover,' Teilhard is reproving me.

'But my cleaning still takes me at least as long as it did my grandmother, and she had no Hoover. And, besides, my Hoover is bust. You lot are no good. I thought you were my friends.' I am conscious that I am beginning to sniffle. 'My last hope is the Institute of Whiteness.'

'What is the Institute of Whiteness?' Blake is both solicitous and genuinely interested.

'The Institute of Whiteness is a body of men and women dedicated to helping housewives combat dirt and evil. They do research and things.'

I have a vision of the Institute – big and gleaming and white – all test-tubes, flow-charts and computer interfaces. All that, but not divorced from the housewife. The Institute is no Shangri La locked away in the Himalayas. It responds directly to the housewife and is dedicated to helping her make her home a better home to live in, up to a hundred per cent more clean. It is the opposite of the Temple of Evil really.

Blake too has a vision of the Institute. It is less favourable than mine.

'Put not your trust in a dead thing, my Angel. Your Institute could only be a cold tomb, a phantastical pyramid built by men whose minds are indexed in marble.'

'Fantastical indeed!' Dickens joins in. 'I do not believe that this Institute exists.'

The others all agree. I, it seems, am the only one ever to have heard of the Institute of Whiteness.

'What evidence for it do you have?'

I tell Darwin about my visit from Dr Hornrim and how interested Dr Hornrim was in my work.

'Did this Hornrim actually say that he was from the Institute of Whiteness?'

'Well no, he didn't, but he was very interested in my work, and what else would he have been doing in my bathroom if he wasn't from the Institute? Oh, and it turns out that his name wasn't Hornrim.'

Darwin taps his nose thoughtfully. I have persuaded no one. Teilhard has a suggestion.

'The existence or not of the Institute of Whiteness is a verifiable hypothesis. Let us look in the London telephone directory.'

We do. My eye anxiously runs down the columns. Institute of Urology. Institute of Welfare Officers. Institute of Woodwork. There is no Institute of Whiteness. It is not possible that they would not have a phone. It is not possible that they would not have a London office. They do not exist. How was it that I was so certain that they did exist?

'So I am on my own, then?'

'We are still with you.'

A hopelessness settles in upon me. The geniuses don't in fact seem to be quite all there in any sense. Their silly game apparently won't stop and while Teilhard and I have been consulting the telephone directory Galton has fallen to the floor groaning realistically. Uncle Darwin pontificates about the wink and the blink or the deliberate non-verbal unit of communication versus the protective reflex action, and about how Killer Wink trains one to make correct deductions from minute signs, which is what science is all about. Blah, blah, blah. Everybody looks distinctly foggy – no, indistinctly foggy, I suppose I mean. They also look frightened. Blake tries to tell me something:

'I saw Bedlam once in the shape of a dish of rotten meat. Then I saw that its doctor had the soul of a blow-fly. It dropped his eggs into the meat. Beware of your doctor, my Angel. Philip is –'

Blake clutches his eyes and slumps backwards.

'Confound me!' cries Dickens. 'I had just decided that it was Blake.'

The four remaining geniuses grin nervously at one another.

'Is it Teilhard, then?' Leonardo hazards.

'Not I,' Teilhard affirms.

'But you would say that, wouldn't you?' Dickens points out.

We are silent, thinking and sniffing. Sniffing. There is a funny smell coming from the corner of the room where De Hooch lies. Suddenly I realize what is going on.

'Let me tell you about the Brothers Karamazov!' I cry. 'Let me tell you how they end.'

And I do ...

'Well, that is the missing sequel to *The Brothers Karamazov*,' I conclude. I could have been talking to myself for all the impression it makes. At length Dickens reluctantly ventures an opinion.

'Marcia, my dear. It is not very good. With all due modesty I must say that it is derivative. Indeed it seeks to imitate my own work, but there is far too much melodrama. This Russian fellow has too little genuine sentiment – if indeed it is by a Russian fellow?' He looks at me inquiringly.

'Oh, you are missing the point. Don't any of you see?' I did not think that they could be so slow. 'I didn't write it and neither did Dostoevsky. Mucor finished Dostoevsky's novel for him, just as he finished your *Edwin Drood* for you. Mucor is a parasite on real literature. He grows on it like dry rot. And now events in this room are following the pattern of events in the ending of *The Brothers Karamazov*.' I point to De Hooch. His corpse is in an advanced state of decomposition. It is decaying far faster than Grushenka's or Zosima's. When a cluster of maggots pops out of an eyeball, I am forced to turn away. 'Do you still not see? You have an extra player in your game and it is no game at all. Mucor is killing you off one by one.'

'I think it is time for us to meet this Mucor.' Darwin is decisive. 'He is a common household mould, I gather?'

'There is nothing common about Mucor.'

But yes, let us leave this room with its mess of egg, corn-flakes, machine oil and corpses – and its stink. My geniuses are fading fast. I want to hurry them on to Mucor, but in the hallway Leonardo is detained by the Hoover. He is fascinated by it and wants it to be explained to him. I tell him that it is broken and that I am too tired and stupid to explain it to him now. But he is not to be put off. He is sure that he can repair it, if only its general principles are explained to him. Dickens is quicker to get the general idea. He is demonstrating how the Hoover works to a baffled Leonardo. In the growing darkness of the hallway I can just make Charles Dickens out. He is crawling along the carpet pretending to suck the dust up with his mouth. Then some dust seems to catch at the back of his throat and, faintly coughing, he expires.

At last Darwin is successful in persuading Leonardo to hurry on towards Mucor. As they kneel over Mucor, a whispering rises from the carpet:

'Death, corruption and turning to dust are the final and therefore the highest forms of humanity.'

For a moment the great bushy white eyebrows of Leonardo and Darwin seem almost to lock together as they stare at each other in wild surmise. Then the great eye of Mucor winks once and these two ghosts of Western culture are blinked out of existence. Everything is fading. Even the corpses and the stink are vanishing. My powers of invention are flagging, failing. I made up these fantasies to get me through a day of boring housework. But soon Philip will be home and I can't take them seriously any more. Even Mucor, still sizzling and hissing away, seems at most a sinister clown. He has never done me any real harm – nor has he been in any position to do so. Boring, all terribly boring. The bed is made, most of the washing up done, half the hall was hoovered, I had a coffee morning (one coffee morning), the living room is more or less tidy. I managed ... as I shall have to manage tomorrow and the day after. I sag against the wall and descend to the floor. I begin to cry.

Mucor is still trying to keep me company, like a faithful old family pet on its last legs:

'Marcia, talk to me. I am your son. I mean it. I am your kith and kin. Listen to me, Marcia. Don't you recognize me? I love you, Mummy. Mummy, did you know that skin flakes are a major component of household dust? I have got your skin flakes in me, you know – and the little mites that feed off your skin flakes. Did you know that in every handful of household dust, there are five thousand such mites? Isn't that interesting, Mummy?'

Piss off, Mucor. That is not what it is all about. I am sitting crying in my house. A leaky faucet is making a tap drip. I can hear it. And the creak of a board as it weakens and settles under the onslaught of woodworm. And flies buzzing over an open jar in the kitchen. There is a carpet-grub in the living room. I didn't imagine that. I know there is wet rot under one of the window-sills. I hope there is no dry rot. Why I should care about these things I do not know, but I cry and I cry. It seems like my own death.

'There is a lot of Philip in me too. Listen to me please, Mummy. Remember that Saturday when Stephanie came round, and you had to go out to the shops and you left Stephanie with Philip in the house? Well, they couldn't even wait to get to the sitting-room sofa. They had it off standing up here in the hallway, and I got some of Philip's semen. All fungi need lots of moisture. Isn't that interesting?'

Enough, Mucor. Enough.

'Please, Mummy. I am talking to you. This is serious. Philip and Stephanie's affair has been going on for ages. Didn't you suspect anything? And yesterday Philip went round to a GP to find out how to get you certified. They are going to put you away, so that they can have the house to themselves. But I'm on your side, Mummy.'

Mucor begins to recite from the missing final stanzas of Spenser's *The Faerie Queene*. It is very faint and it sounds as though he is trying to keep his courage up.

> '... to be behoven,
> The Genius fell for Mucor's stroke was lustie.
> Greisie, drearie, wearie, mustie, rustie,
> In darkling night she lay in Castle Sloven,
> Whylome her paramour Philip was not trustie.
>
> Whyleare with hands so softe they did not dishes
> Seemingly, she beat upon the Sauvage Carpet as it was hight,
> And as she bate, so she despeired at the messe upon
>   its stitches,
>   For there it spread its filthe in Heaven's despyte,
>   Performing dwarfish antic Marcia to affright.
>   Thought the drudge in the Chambered Mind
>   Toiling allwhyles at Dark Mucor's delyte.
>   Seek out the hallway and ye shall find
>   Household mould and maide entwyned.
>
>   Now hear the clamour of the dolorous stroke ...'

It is one work of literature he will not finish. There is a bell ringing. My eyes are such a blur that I can hardly see to reach for the phone. No, it is not the phone. Someone is at the door. The ringing has stopped and there are fumbling sounds. The lock is turning.

'Sorry, dear. I couldn't find my key for a moment.'

'Ooooh, Philip!' I reach out my arms to hug him and draw him down on to the floor, but he pulls away and through the mist of my tears I see that Stephanie is standing behind him, and then I see that 'Dr Hornrim' is with them too. Are those meant to be reassuring smiles?

'Don't cry, my love.' Taking one of my hands, Stephanie settles herself down on the hallway carpet beside me. More oddly, 'Dr Hornrim' takes the other hand and lowers himself down on my other side. Philip towers above us. He does not seem to know where to look. He takes a fleck of dandruff from his jacket shoulder and affects to contemplate it with minute attention, but I can see that, under his lids, he is watching me watching him. Stephanie gives my hand a squeeze, but I turn the other way.

'You are not from the Institute of Whiteness, are you? And I know that your name is not Hornrim.'

'The name is White actually. I'm a GP. Tell me about this Institute of Whiteness.'

It is hard for me to get going. It all sounds so silly, especially telling my husband. But eventually I do, and I tell them everything I told the geniuses and more.

' – but there is no such thing as the Institute of Whiteness . . .' I tail off miserably.

'There is no such thing as the Institute of Whiteness,' Dr White echoes me.

Do they think me an idiot, that I cannot see the glances they are exchanging? The eyes of Philip and Stephanie are signalling Dr White that he will have to speak for them.

'Marcia, my dear, I want you to listen to me very carefully,' he says. 'When you were a child you had the sensation that the adults were keeping something from you. You may not have said so. You may not even have told yourself this suspicion, but it was there. It was one of your assumptions about life. There is nothing odd about this. Many children entertain similar suspicions. Then, when you were a little older – say, about ten – you probably put this only dimly formulated suspicion behind you, and you settled into family life, school activities and so on. Later yet, in adolescence, you may have concluded that the great secret was the facts of life. There is usually a sense of anticlimax then. That's a very common feeling, for sex isn't such a great thing after all, and many people whose sex lives are not all that they should be are able to lead lives that are in other respects perfectly fulfilling.'

He coughs. He is so nervous. It is not at all like his visit earlier in the day.

'Now, Marcia, you see the hand that Philip is stretching out to you? There is a piece of dandruff on it. I want you to look at that piece of dandruff and tell me what you see. It is very small, just there.'

If that is what he wants, then he is going to get it. I gaze into Philip's palm and speak:

'I'm used to working with larger flakes of dandruff, but they are all interesting, aren't they? I like dandruff. There is an immense amount of it in household dust, and it makes the dust seem less alien – gives it a human face I suppose. Looking at this little bit here, I can see that it is more symmetrical than the big ones I'm used to. Every small particle of dandruff has its own distinctive structure, like a snowflake or a fingerprint. If this is an exam, then I am going to fail it – I just haven't thought long enough about small bits of dandruff. Besides, the light is terribly dim in the hallway. This particular bit is like a five-gated city. Don't laugh – but now, looking at it, I have the weirdest feeling that this is the little grain of dust in Lambeth that Satan could not find, and the reason he could not find it is that Philip took it away with him this morning. I see an immense world of delight in this piece of dandruff. It is indeed a lovely heaven. Don't laugh.'

'No one is laughing,' says White gently. 'And you haven't failed any exam.'

He lets the silence build up before he speaks again.

'Marcia, I have to tell you that there is indeed a great secret which until now has been kept from you –'

'Welcome to the team!' Stephanie cuts in enthusiastically, but White shushes her, and goes on:

'Look at us, Marcia. Dry those tears. Well, don't look at us if you don't want to, but picture us if you like. Picture us as extraterrestrial beings who for a long time have been circling the planet in our flying saucers keeping it under covert surveillance, waiting to see – to see when that planet's civilization shall have achieved sufficient maturity for us to admit it into the Pangalactic Civilization.'

Now I do look up and, seeing the expression on my face, he hastens on.

'No, we are not mad and neither are you. You, Marcia, are the planet, we are the extra-terrestrials in our flying saucers and now we are making contact with you. We think that you are ready. I'm sorry, perhaps the metaphor is confusing. I'm afraid I'm rather fond of metaphors. We all of us here are. Oh dear, how can I explain ...? You see, there is no Institute of Whiteness. There never could be.'

'It would attract too much attention – and too many idiots,' Philip interrupts.

'Quite so,' White continues. 'But while a big official institute with a known address is out of the question, something more informal does exist, and has existed for centuries. Leonardo da Vinci and Isaac Newton may well have been members. However we keep no records. No names, no pack-drill. Today we are a loosely organized group of like-minded people, thousands of us, who meet from time to time to exchange notes and perceptions. Of course there is nothing sinister about what we do. The general public would simply find our researches extremely dull and (let us be realistic) somewhat ridiculous. But, as I put it to myself, there is nothing trivial about minutiae, nor is the trivial so unimportant. My own interest is in dirty handkerchiefs, Stephanie specializes in the patterns made by grease stains on the bottom of pans, and Philip, rather unusually, compares the smells of drains. You seem to us a good all-rounder.'

Stephanie's enthusiasm can be controlled no longer:

'Did you see the folds on my skirt this morning? Weren't they super! I knew that you had spotted them. Perhaps you would like to write a report on them for us?'

'We have safe houses and we do circulate reports,' White presses on. 'Sometimes we even publish reports, if we are sure that they are not going to attract attention, in odd places like *Good Housekeeping*. Philip here has been pressing for you to join us ever since your marriage.'

'Philip?' I look at him doubtfully.

'Why do you think I married you, you silly darling?' He kneels down to give me a great big hug.

White coughs and doggedly continues:

'It fell to Stephanie to do the independent vetting. I may say that her report was entirely favourable. And then of course I came round this afternoon to do the final check (that was a wonderful understain, by the way). Well, what do you say? Will you join us?'

'I don't know what to say.' My voice is all chokey.

'Say yes!' they chorus.

'Yes, then. Look, it is silly us all sitting here on the carpet. Let's go into the kitchen and I will make some tea.'

Pausing only to point out the played-out body of Mucor sprawled in the hallway, I lead them into the kitchen. Through the blur of my moist eyes the kitchen appears as a glittering paradise. While I get the tea things ready I tell them all about my day's housework, with Stephanie filling in with some of the details about the coffee morning. I tell them about my last adventure with Darwin and Leonardo and they all laugh, but they are laughing with me, not at me.

'Gosh!' says Stephanie. 'When I clean my house I have similar things going with Fu Manchu and P. T. Barnum, but nothing half so intellectual as your lot.' She is really impressed.

Dr White smiles with a genial warmth I could not previously have suspected him of possessing.

'Look, this calls for a celebration. A friend of mine has got some dirty handkerchiefs together for me at the hospital in the middle of town. Why don't we all go there and have a look at them, and then go on to dinner out? Dinner with champagne!'

I tell them I have to get ready. Actually, I run upstairs clutching the little fleck of dandruff that Philip has given me. It is the key that has unlocked all our hearts and I place it carefully in the centre of my jewel-box. Darwin was dead all right, but there was a whole new world waiting for me when I came downstairs.

Out in the street, we all link arms and, as I look up the street, I can see no stain on the horizon of my future happiness.